Praise for R. G. Alexander's *Regina in the Sun*

"Regina in the Sun is a wonderful twist on the vampire myth and R.G. Alexander is a born storyteller. Ms. Alexander pulls such emotion out of me with just a few words that I can go from joyously happy to heart wrenchingly sad in a matter of minutes. Regina in the Sun has such heart that I can feel the words pulsing with every beat."

~ *Joyfully Reviewed*

Rating: 5 hearts "R.G. Alexander creates a dark sensual world that will fascinate readers by weaving a magical spell to tempt and seduce the senses."

~ *The Romance Studio*

Rating: 5 Nymphs "Children of the Goddess Book 1: Regina in the Sun is so well written you can't help but love the actions of Regina and Zander throughout the story. R. G. Alexander has done a fabulous job and I am impatiently waiting to read the next."

~ *Literary Nymphs*

Look for these titles by
R. G. Alexander

Now Available:

Children of the Goddess Series
Regina in the Sun (Book 1)
Lux in Shadow (Book 2)

Not in Kansas

Coming Soon:

Surrender Dorothy

Regina in the Sun

R. G. Alexander

A Samhain Publishing, Ltd. publication.

Samhain Publishing, Ltd.
577 Mulberry Street, Suite 1520
Macon, GA 31201
www.samhainpublishing.com

Regina in the Sun
Copyright © 2009 by R. G. Alexander
Print ISBN: 978-1-60504-114-8
Digital ISBN: 1-59998-924-7

Editing by Bethany Morgan
Cover by Anne Cain

First Samhain Publishing, Ltd. electronic publication: April 2008
First Samhain Publishing, Ltd. print publication: February 2009

Dedication

For Cookie—Love is the reason. And to my smutketeers, divas and deviants, especially Kristen. If she hadn't let me into her "clan", there would be no Regina. Last but never least—Beth—your support and belief can never be repaid. Thank you.

Chapter One

She was going to die.

It wasn't because of the Were following her, though he could have easily killed her several times over since she'd started running. It hadn't taken Regina long to realize the sadistic jerk was simply enjoying the chase—toying with her like the weakened prey she had become.

He was too cocky, confident that she couldn't escape him, and she'd used that against him. He'd fallen behind and he'd never get to her in time. She was too close to her destination. She hoped.

She raced through the night with inhuman speed. Only one of her own would notice that she wasn't as swift as she should have been. The injuries she'd received a few weeks ago were slowing her down.

Her wounds, the narrow cobblestone streets of the small English town—even the snow that fell wet and heavy from the sky barely fazed her as she passed. She had to reach safety soon. *Sanctuary.* Only then would she be able to rest.

Reggie wanted to laugh at the irony. Here she was, running from one enemy directly into the arms of another. But this time it was the devil she *didn't* know that seemed the safer bet.

All she had to go on were the stories her sire, Elizabeth, would share whenever she was melancholy. Liz had lived near here with her husband until his brutal death at the hands of a pack of renegade Weres.

The son of the sanctuary's proprietor had helped Liz escape and get back on her feet after the terrible loss. She still talked about him with fondness, and Reggie could only hope he would aid her as well, even though she was Unborn.

She slowed as she came upon a large grey building with no windows. A sign dangled over her head. Forming the shape of a black shield with a red lion rampant, the words "Ye Olde Haven Pub" were carved beneath the paws. Haven. That's what Liz had called it. This must be the place.

Regina took a deep breath and tried to steel her spine. She had heard of the intolerance, the dangers inherent in what she was about to do. She was an Unborn, created by another and not of pure, or *Trueblood,* lineage.

Her entire clan was made up of the misfits of the Vampire world. All Unborn, mostly females, they had banded together to form their own community. It was a community based on tolerance, and the first place Reggie had ever been accepted for exactly who she was. The first place she'd felt safe. The Deva Clan was her family. That was why she had to do this.

She *was* going to die. But before she did, she had to make sure her family would be protected from the demon on her tail. She had to find Lux Sariel. Had to plead with his father, the mediator for all the Trueblood clans, to put aside prejudice long enough to stop *Les Loups De L'Ombre,* The Shadow Wolves, from destroying everything she loved.

The unassuming and plain exterior had fooled her into expecting the same inside. From what she could see, she could have been in the most exclusive club in New York, instead of a tiny, out of the way village in Norwich.

The place was a wonder. She looked around slowly, the

darkness of the pub a blessing to her kind. Softly lit sconces were placed strategically throughout the room, and small candles graced the center of each booth and table, but there was no garish lighting to spoil the mood or hurt the sensitive eyes of the pub's unique clientele.

Black leather booths framed the walls, leaving no one's back vulnerable to the door in what she was sure was more for defense than decoration. The large room was separated into three sections by the different elevations of the dark wood flooring.

From where she stood in the center doorway, one step up would take her to the majority of the booths, which had polished tables and plush seating and were wide enough for several people to comfortably recline. They faced a medium-sized dance floor looking up at a small, well-lit stage, currently occupied by a single musician playing acoustic guitar.

To the left, a step down would take her to a small grouping of even wider booths that sat directly across from a very impressive-looking and well-stocked bar set against the far wall. The long, polished countertop was laced with ornate carvings etched in silver and gold. Several empty swivel stools lined the bar, leaving her a clear path to navigate.

The pub gave off an air of luxurious elegance, though it felt neither cold nor intimidating. The warm tones and comfortable ambiance seemed to welcome her, drawing her in. She could see why the place was so popular with humans and Vampires alike.

The decor was oddly familiar. The carvings on the crown molding that mirrored those on the bar and the pot-bellied stove in the corner reminded her of the main family room at Castle Deva. She wondered if Liz had done that on purpose. Reggie felt a wave of longing for the home she'd shared with the others of her clan on the shores of Lago Maggiore. She squashed down the feelings before they could consume her.

Standing in the entryway between the two separated areas, she trembled with adrenaline and pain. Now that she was here, so close to achieving her goal, she felt the weeks of sleeplessness, hunger and fear crashing over her in a relentless wave that had her weaving on her feet.

It was easy to sense the emotions of everyone in the crowded bar, the exact instant that they all realized an Unborn stranger had entered their territory. She walked as steadily as possible to the bar, her eyes straight ahead as she focused on the wary bartender.

The musician on the stage kept playing, but Reggie knew that all eyes were turned her way as she ordered a shot of whiskey to warm her frozen limbs. She knocked it back before speaking to the bartender in what she hoped was a confident tone.

"I need to speak to Lux Sariel."

The man stilled before nodding sharply, disappearing behind a panel door leading to the back. She closed her eyes and tried to quiet the turmoil in her mind.

Suspicion, disbelief and the unmistakable feeling of malice bore down on her from all sides. Reggie used her unique abilities to block them all out, just as she had blocked out the worried thoughts of her clan when they had tried to find her, to help her.

Blessed internal silence. *At last.* And then she recognized it.

The music.

The first smile to grace her face since this whole nightmare began curved her lips. The dark curly hair and large soulful eyes staring back at her from the stage were easily discernible. It was him. One of her favorite musicians.

She didn't stop to wonder how or why such a sought-after artist was playing solo in a pub filled with creatures of the night. Liz had once had Elvis himself to the castle to play for Madame Nicolette's birthday. In fact, that was the year she'd decided to change her name to Lisa Marie, though that phase hadn't lasted long.

So Reggie didn't question. She simply reveled in the sad and soulful voice, the haunting guitar that reminded her of lazy afternoons and peaceful evenings with her birth mother's family. She sent out a silent mental request to the man on stage as the last few chords faded and, without hesitation, the notes of her favorite song began to fill the air.

She walked towards the dance floor, a bit delirious from exhaustion and heedless of the surprised murmurs, and began to sway to the poignant melody.

In her mind's eye she was young again, free of pain as her grandmother taught her how to story-dance. That's what she'd always called it. Daj Mia believed that every dance should tell a story.

Reggie's body instinctively followed the movements she'd learned so long ago, before she knew that a world beyond her human family's tents existed. Before she knew that all the monsters and magick in her Daj's fireside stories were real.

Her hands rose above her head. Wrists and hips rolled smoothly as she twirled to the slow, sad ballad.

The song told of a girl who didn't seem to fit in the world. Lost in darkness and pain, the only freedom—only happiness she knew—was in the sun.

The irony of the lyrics weren't lost on Reggie. She was a Vampire, after all. And yet, it was nothing but the truth. The last true memories she had of love and laughter were brilliant with the light of day.

As the words wove around her, she could almost believe she was dancing in the sun, could feel it on her face. Centuries of darkness were erased in a heartbeat. Lost in the magic of the song, she could feel the dew-filled grass beneath her thinly covered feet instead of the hard wood of the pub floor. It was her family's laughing eyes, shining with support and approval, gazing at her as she swayed instead of the cold judgment of the strangers who watched her every move.

The waif-like creature danced as if she were in another world. He realized she didn't comprehend the effect she was having on her paralyzed audience. Several of his clientele stood, their intentions clear. They planned to remove the unwanted element from their midst, but something about the solitary dancer froze them in their tracks. A sadness they all recognized, a yearning some of them had never known and a sexuality that held them captive.

He couldn't tear his gaze away as her belly rolled and she arched her back, the movements beyond graceful, unknowingly sensual. Her hips jutted sharply left and right, body undulating like water.

The air left his lungs, desire racing through his limbs, weighing them down. Her waist-length blue-black tresses swept the floor as her neck rolled forward. She reached up once more, her face glowing with some inner light as she embraced a vision only she could see.

She was mesmerizing.

The beauty fell to her knees, back lowering until it touched the floor as the final words to the song echoed through the silent room.

It was then that he noticed her haggard appearance. The torn clothing, the scrapes covering her arms and the extreme pallor of her skin made his gut clench.

A tear fell unchecked down her cheek. He tensed as if to go to her, but his brother rushed past him to her side. Lux picked the girl up as if she were light as a feather and whispered softly in her ear. He joined them in time to hear the low, sultry voice tremble in response.

"Elizab-eth said... Sanctu—" She passed out before she could finish the sentence.

Lux looked up at him in surprise before holding the girl protectively closer.

"Sanctuary, Zander. She's asking for sanctuary."

The murmurs had picked up around them. He and his brother looked over the crowd, sensing the growing agitation. Those who had stood before seemed to have shaken themselves out of their hypnotic stupor, stepping forward as if to protest. Zander moved closer to his brother and the unconscious girl in his arms. "It's the law. Sanctuary has been requested and cannot be refused."

Half the crowd nodded, intimidated by the large proprietor and still moved by the scene they'd just witnessed. The rest of them Zander ignored. Directing Lux towards his rooms and instructing the remaining employees to keep alert, he quickly followed the pair upstairs.

His curiosity, his protective instincts, and something he wasn't quite ready to name were all in overdrive as he thought of the beautiful, mysterious stranger in his brother's arms. Who was she? And why did he have the feeling his life would never be the same?

"Who is she?"

Zander Sariel looked down at Lux. His younger brother

sighed and ran his hands through his shoulder-length burgundy hair. "From what she said and the traces I'm sensing, I assume she's one of Elizabeth's. A member of the Deva Clan."

Zander felt his face twisting in a tired grimace as he realized what Lux was saying. Not just any Unborn, his little sleeping beauty belonged to Liz, the widow of one of his dearest friends, and a long-time pain in his ass.

How many Truebloods had complained over the years about her growing clan of "dangerous" Unborns?

That his people were a little pompous and paranoid was the understatement of the millennium. He didn't share their opinions, but since taking his father's place as glorified diplomat and Mediator a few hundred years before, he had to listen with objectivity. Regardless of his own beliefs.

Zander knew Elizabeth well. Lux had helped her sire and husband, Malcolm, keep her hidden during their marriage. Zander had even helped his younger brother get her out of harm's way with enough funds to last her several lifetimes after the tragedy of his old friend's untimely death. He'd owed that to Malcolm.

But he couldn't ignore how Liz and her rash acts of vengeance and regular creation of new Unborns had affected the balance of his community. And now one of her "children" was lying on his bed, obviously wounded and publicly asking for help.

"I'll take full responsibility for her." He heard Lux state quietly as he looked down at the fragile creature.

She seemed so helpless, ethereal as a dream. Exactly the type the softhearted Lux had always felt compelled to protect. He placed a strong hand on Lux's shoulder, drawing his brother's gaze.

"She's mine." He was startled by the sound of his own

voice. "I mean—my responsibility. She asked for sanctuary. It's mine to give."

He looked at her for a moment, sitting on the bed beside her to brush a wayward hair behind her ear. The strand was shocking silver against the black, strange to see in one of their kind, especially one so young.

Though pale with pain and exhaustion, the girl was entrancing. Long lashes hid her eyes, but he recalled their exotic tilt and the glint of gold as she'd danced. Her face was narrow, almost feline, cheekbones sharp with dramatic hollows that could easily have been caused by hunger.

An ebony-colored bindu marked her forehead, between elegantly arched brows. The symbol tickled the edges of his memory, but he was distracted as his gaze was drawn to her incredibly kissable mouth. The lower lip was fuller and kept her mouth in a perpetual pout, as if inviting him, even in sleep, to taste.

Zander could sense the illness in her, regardless of his distraction, but he wasn't sure of the cause. His usual calm seemed to abandon him as he felt some nameless emotion render him helpless.

"What's wrong with her?" Zander watched intently as Lux, who sat on her other side, took her hand in his and closed his eyes. Whereas Zander had been trained from birth to take his father's place as leader of his clan and Mediator of the Clan Trust, his younger brother had always been a natural healer, possessing so strong a gift that he'd been hand-picked by the High Priestess, Glynn Magriel, herself.

The Healers were an ancient link to the long-forgotten past, rarely used and, many believed, no longer necessary in this day and age. Zander knew how important it had been to Lux, and he'd had the worst argument of his life with their father in an

17

attempt to allow his brother to continue his apprenticeship before the decision had ultimately been made.

Unfortunately, as a member of the prestigious Sariel family, Lux had been forced to leave his training and focus on the family business. As Zander's second-in-command, he was given a higher status, respect and power in his community.

It meant nothing to Lux, and Zander knew it, but his brother had agreed for his sake. Until he was mated and had a child of his own, insuring the continuation of the Mediator line, Lux's presence would be required. The Trust had demanded that caveat from the powerful Sariels for generations.

Vampire politics was a long way from the calling of Lux's heart, but he had dealt with it fairly well, at least outwardly. He told Zander he took comfort in the knowledge that healing could be accomplished in many different ways.

But Lux's true healing abilities and knowledge would help this wounded beauty tonight. Zander had no idea why it meant so much to him. Still, he could not deny that it did.

When Lux let go of her hand and began to unbutton her ragged blouse, Zander grabbed his wrist and glared.

Lux rolled his eyes. "She's injured. Someone used dark magick to mark her. It's familiar, but I'm not sure why. It's draining her life force and I have to find the entry point. You can leave if it's too much for your puritanical sensibilities."

Zander's jaw tightened with understanding as he began to help in the removal of the dirty fabric. He tried to be as clinical as his brother, but as her flesh was revealed, Zander felt an answering response send a tremor through his body. She was a goddess.

Completely dressed she could pass for an adolescent, but beneath the loose-fitting blouse and torn jeans, she was a deliciously petite armful.

Full, ripe breasts topped with dark cocoa nipples beaded in the cold air of the room. He took in the cream-colored curves and softly rounded hips. He had the sudden urge to caress them until he could thread his fingers through the neat triangle of ebony curls below.

There was another tattoo, low on her pelvis, this one of a small tribal sun. The symbol made him smile. He could practically feel it against his tongue as he imagined laving her silken skin from head to toe.

Hard with desire, he had to shake himself out of his lustful thoughts as Lux began to turn her body on its side in search of the wound. She had asked for his help, he reminded himself harshly, not this inappropriate and shameless voyeurism.

All thoughts of lust disappeared as he caught sight of it on the left side of her lower back. It looked like someone had gouged out a chunk of her flesh.

Zander moved to the side so Lux could examine her. She was covered in fading bruises and deep scratches, but it was the large gash on her back that held his attention. The edges were charred with markings that chilled him to the bone.

Confusion and fear clawed at his gut. Why hadn't the tissue mended? One of the blessings of their kind, Unborn or True, was the ability to heal swiftly from any physical wound.

As long as their hearts and heads remained attached, they could, at the very least, *begin* their own healing process. Did she need blood?

The girl immediately stirred and turned towards Zander. "No blood. Shadow Wolf...too dangerous. No blood."

She looked distraught and Lux made soft soothing sounds until she calmed. One golden eye opened and tried to focus past the pain. "Liz—danger...Lux...save them...let me—"

Lux had placed his hand on her forehead, using his ability

19

to send waves of reassurance and sleep her way. The girl appeared to struggle against him for a moment, but she soon slipped into unconsciousness, obviously too weak to put up much of a fight.

Save them. Let me die.

That was the request she hadn't been allowed to finish. And her broken, nearly incoherent speech had set off alarms in Zander's mind. Shadow Wolf? Had she been injured by a member of the *Shadow*?

He remembered all the tension-filled nights and emergency meetings his father had been a part of during the final stages of the war between Vampires and Shadow Wolves. Most of the major battles had been finished long before he was born—but that was over six hundred and sixty three years ago.

The Shadow were Weres that, until now, were thought to have been exterminated. Beings of unbelievable strength and cruelty, they'd harnessed the powers of black magick along with their natural abilities in order to wreak chaos on the Vampire and human population alike. Had the Trust been misinformed?

Lux covered her with a light blanket at her hips, tracing the blackened edge of the jagged wound and drawing Zander's attention to it once more. "This is at least a few weeks old, but instead of healing, it's killing the surrounding tissue. Do you see these markings? It's a powerful and ancient spell meant to counteract a Vampire's natural healing abilities. Whoever did this wanted to slow her down and cause her pain. I don't think they wanted to kill her outright."

Zander clenched his fists in fury at her unknown assailant. "She said 'No blood...too dangerous.' What did she mean?"

Lux sighed. "When I studied with Glynn, she told me a bespelled wound from a Shadow Wolf could be poisonous to other Vampires. To taste of the victim's blood, or to allow any of their saliva or fluids to taint your bloodstream, would be to share their fate."

He paused and Zander could almost see the wheels turning in his mind. "Although she did say the fatality rate was higher in Unborns. The purer the blood, the stronger the immunity." He began rolling up his sleeve and moving closer to the tiny figure huddled on the massive bed.

"What are you doing?"

"It just occurred to me. There is no purer blood than ours. It's the reason our family was designated for mediation. The Sariels are pure Vampires, natural-born—every one of them. So far the fact has meant less than nothing to me, but it might actually be worth a great deal in this situation."

A rumbling growl rose from Zander's chest as Lux placed his arm around the girl. His brother raised his eyebrows at the sound, a curious expression on his face.

"I'll do it. You're the best healer I know. If something happens, you're the only one who'd know what to do." The compliment, given through gritted teeth, didn't exactly sound sincere.

Zander meant every word, but it wasn't the whole truth. All he knew was the sight of another hand, even his brother's, on her flesh was bringing out a possessiveness he'd never felt before. He wanted to be the one to touch her, to save her. Hell, he just wanted *her*. Badly.

"Don't give me that look, *little* brother. I'm the only logical choice." Zander avoided the knowing blue eyes as he reached back to pull his shirt over his head, tossing it on the ground before returning to the bed.

Lux smiled innocently. "Actually, you're the least logical choice. If you become ill while trying to save a *worthless* little Unborn, how will the clan heads react? Dad is officially retired

21

and he and mom are currently out of contact on their second...or is it third honeymoon? And I am not exactly up to snuff when it comes to keeping those hyenas from ripping each other apart."

Zander felt his expression tighten when Lux called the girl worthless. His brother had no sense of self-preservation, he thought, as he watched Lux's smile widen further.

He knew that Lux hadn't a prejudiced bone in his body. He had always argued *against* the Unborn restrictions. He still corresponded with Elizabeth on a regular basis, hardly the actions of a prejudiced Trueblood. But Zander wasn't feeling rational. He felt restless, needy. And Lux's attempts to bait him weren't helping.

The younger man moved out of the way without another word as Zander replaced Lux's arm with his own. He slid completely onto the bed, taking the petite bundle fully into his embrace.

So fragile. So heartrendingly beautiful that she stole his breath. He moved them into a position where Lux could keep an eye on her wound.

As his brother gathered his supply of healing herbs from his apartment down the hall, Zander examined every curve of her face. She was frowning, the space between her elegant brows crinkled up as if in confusion. Or pain.

He sent up a little prayer that he would be up to the challenge, that his blood and Lux's gift for healing would be enough to save her.

Lux handed him a vial of amber liquid. "I want you to take this tincture. It should ensure that you suffer nothing more than something resembling a bad hangover...*if* Glynn was right about the rest."

Zander downed the foul-tasting medicine. He grimaced,

lifting his forearm to his mouth and biting down with his sharp incisors to open the vein there. He placed it against the prone girl's lips.

When she didn't immediately take his offering, Lux laid his hand on her head, mentally compelling her to drink. Zander's fingers gently caressed her throat, attempting to induce her to swallow. It took both of them to force her compliance. The sheer strength of her mind was astounding.

Her open mouth firmed on Zander's arm as she began to down the life-giving liquid with needy gulps. An unexpected side effect took Zander by surprise.

Though Vampires always considered the sharing of blood a sensual if not outright sexual act, never before had he experienced the fire now shooting through his veins. The erection he'd been trying to tame hardened to a painful degree, his eyes closing with the force of his desire as he concentrated on the feel of her full lips greedily wrapped around his flesh.

He forgot Lux's presence, the girl's illness, even his own name for a moment. All he knew was that he had to touch her, had to taste her in return. It was an instinct he couldn't deny. Pushing her hair to the side and lifting her higher against his chest, Zander sunk his fangs into her neck. It was too late for Lux to stop him as he gorged himself on her taste.

The dark magick attacked immediately. An evil sentience that was even now trying to maintain its grip on her soul reached for him with an angry roar.

He pushed it aside, focusing his entire being on the woman beneath him. Just below the darkness lay the richest, sweetest flavor he'd ever known. Like starlight and summer and wildflowers. Like peace and laughter. The essence that was...*Regina*.

Zander felt doorways beginning to click open in his mind,

his muscles going rigid as a flood of information washed over his consciousness.

Where he had been alone he now felt a quiet presence. He reached out to touch it, to touch her. His *grathita*. His blood-bound mate. Now the reason for his instantaneous lust, for his sudden possessiveness, was clear.

Regina was his...in the most elemental way possible. She was the other half of his soul. That was the only explanation for the new knowledge and awareness in his mind. Why he could hear her thoughts as well as his own, sense her spirit strengthening with the gift of his blood. He was overcome by the discovery. At last, he thought.

At last.

He began to weaken and he lifted his head from her neck with a last lingering lick. She moaned, protesting his absence, even in her unconscious state. His body was shaking by the time she released his arm and slipped into a deep and healing sleep. Zander closed the wound himself, taking another drink of his brother's tonic and listening to Lux's low chants before lying back in exhaustion, his woman securely wrapped in his arms. He felt a hand on his brow and he smiled.

"Regina. Her name is Regina."

Chapter Two

Reggie had a hangover. At least, that's what it felt like. Either that or two irate and frustrated little gnomes were taking turns using her head as a ping-pong ball. She lay as still as possible, trying to get her bearings while praying for the gnomes to get bored with her and decide to pester someone else.

The last thing she remembered was...*Haven*. She'd made it. She'd actually gotten there and, if she was remembering correctly, she'd spoken to Lux.

Her shoulders relaxed and the banging began to fade as relief rushed in. Elizabeth and the others would be safe now. She just knew it. And she could continue with her plans without regret or guilt at knowing she'd almost been responsible for a catastrophe.

"I think a slight change in plans might be in order."

She froze at the sound of the voice. It was close. A little *too* close. Almost as if it was coming from—she groaned in silent mortification as a large, masculine arm slid around her bare waist. What did she do last night?

A male chuckle washed over her. The arm, already causing a tingling heat to spread across her skin, squeezed her gently. "You didn't do anything, Regina. You were hurt and we took you upstairs to tend to your wounds."

The gnomes were renewing their efforts with gusto. He knew her name. *And* what she'd been thinking. He shouldn't be able to read her thoughts so clearly. He shouldn't be able to read her at all.

She tried to block him, a gift she'd always taken for granted and rarely had to use, but she could sense his amused patience at her attempt. She didn't stop to think that she might be able to read him in return, her fear turning to anger as she raised up on her elbow, whipping around to confront him.

Her brain registered several facts at once. The first being the pain in her side that, while it still stung, was dramatically less than it had been only yesterday. Secondly, she was lying naked beside quite possibly the sexiest man she'd ever seen. Her eyes glazed and her mouth watered with desire as she slowly looked him over.

Once.

Pause.

Twice.

Okay, perhaps sexy was too weak of a word. But he wasn't beautiful. She wouldn't even say he was exceptionally handsome. He looked too hard for that. Too raw and elemental and male.

He lay above the covers in unbuttoned black dress pants and nothing else. His thighs bulged as if trying to escape their cloth prison, and she knew instinctively that this man had to have clothes created just to fit him.

A fine line of hair disappeared beneath the lowered zipper, where another growing and rather impressive bulge looked as if it might be planning its escape. Her gaze flew upward swiftly, past the enviable six-pack, up to the smooth, hairless pecs and along the tightly corded neck before working up her courage to face her mysterious bed partner.

Short, sandy hair looking a bit tousled from sleep framed a strong jaw, sharp cheekbones and a regal nose. It was a face that was saved from being too harsh by the hint of dimples, which appeared when his firm lips tilted slightly at her scrutiny.

Eyes the color of blazing sapphires narrowed with desire and obvious intent. She suddenly recalled that this man had been able to read her thoughts. That was why she'd turned in the first place. She tilted her chin, ignoring the blush heating her cheeks, determined to retain her righteous indignation even in the face of such edible eye candy.

His blue eyes widened in shock before he rolled onto his back with a surprised shout of laughter. *"Edible eye candy?"*

His rude guffawing was cut short with an "Oomph!" as she whacked him with the nearest pillow. She started to get up, determined to escape the gorgeous mind-reading lunatic, only to find herself trapped beneath him while he grinned in amusement, utterly ignoring her warning glare.

"Regina," he murmured as he focused his attention on her full lower lip. "If you're saying you find me attractive, then let me just tell you that the feeling is entirely mutual."

His head lowered slowly, giving her ample time to reject his advance. On any other day, she would have been stunned by her own inaction. She couldn't seem to move. Not even when she felt the first touch of his lips on hers.

Their fingers laced together above her head, the gentle restraint adding to her arousal. He took his time, torturing her with featherlight kisses and gentle nips.

The strange, sweet intimacy of the moment stretched out until she found herself straining her neck to get closer, her mouth opening in invitation. Greedy for more of the delicious stranger's kiss.

He sucked her lower lip between his teeth, biting gently

before soothing the sting away with his tongue. She gasped with arousal and he pulled back to look into her eyes for a heartbeat. Angling his head, he took her mouth in a soul-consuming kiss that had her moaning wantonly into his mouth. The sound encouraged him to taste her more fully, their tongues sparring for control in her mouth as he shifted his hardening erection into the apex of her thighs.

She wrapped her lips around his tongue, sucking him deeper into her mouth. He jerked against her, and then he was reciprocating in a way that made her entire body tremble. On and on, lips and fangs and tongues warred for supremacy in a sensual battle that neither wanted to end.

Never had she experienced anything like the need that flooded through her from the first touch of his lips. He was like a narcotic, drugging her limbs and causing her heart to beat a panicked tattoo against her breast. His taste was both darkly mysterious and achingly familiar. His lips burned against hers with a blaze like the noonday sun, so hot she was sure she'd melt beneath him.

He thrust his hips gently against her sex and even through the sheet that separated them she felt an answering rush of arousal dampen her thighs. She'd never imagined she could be so close to coming from a kiss. A hot, unbearably sexy kiss, but a kiss nonetheless.

He groaned as she arched against him in return and she reveled in the knowledge that his desire was just as strong as hers. That he wanted her, his *grathita*, more than he'd ever wanted another. She was *his* and he would—

She must be sensing his thoughts. Picking up on them as if they were her own. At the same moment the realization struck her, he pressed his body fully against hers, causing her to cry out in pain at the forgotten injury.

He leapt off her as if he were on fire, the lust in his eyes turning quickly to worry. Kneeling on the bed, he bent to check her mending wound, ignoring the hand that tried to slap him away.

"I'm really going to have to work on my timing."

The wry voice caused the two to jump apart, startled. Reggie felt her cheeks heat as the man she'd just been groping leaned his back against the bed frame with a sigh, subtly trying to cover Regina's naked frame with the blanket, hiding her from the other man's view.

Without a word she jerked the fabric from his hands, pulling the cover up to her neck defensively. She looked towards the glorious creature standing at the edge of the bed, the memory of being carried from the dance floor surfacing in her mind. This was Lux.

He held up the overflowing bag in his hand, which showed the name of a well-known clothing store. "I brought you something to wear. Your other clothing was, well, unsalvageable."

He waited for her to accept his offering, but she merely nodded her thanks and looked at him pointedly until he turned his head and shut his eyes.

She reached out with her mind and gasped at the amusement hiding in Lux's thoughts, as well as the memory of undressing her after she'd collapsed. At her sound of outrage, Lux spun his head back around, looking towards her in shock before glancing at the other man—*his brother*, Reggie suddenly realized—for an explanation.

"I don't know why you're looking at him. Just ask me." She crossed her arms over the blanket that she had wrapped around her, realizing her breasts were plumping over the edge when Lux couldn't seem to tear his gaze away from the view.

Her golden eyes rolled and she shook her head. "After all the stories Liz told me, I thought you'd be a bit more, well, genteel."

The charming smile Lux had been wearing since he'd arrived turned sinful, causing her to shiver at the change. "Genteel? Ahhh. Well, yes, I like men if that's what you're inferring. But that doesn't mean I don't enjoy women just as thoroughly. Especially when they have such undeniably charming...assets."

Reggie turned away with a blush to see the object of her recent lust sprawled casually on the rumpled bed, a sensual smile on his face.

"Of the two, Lux is far more notorious than I, Regina mine. Ask anyone. No one's safe when he's on the prowl." The two men laughed together as she huffed and grabbed the clothing bag, storming past them to the bathroom, her face beet red. Before she closed the door, she turned.

"To answer your question, Lux, I'm a Reader. A telepath. And I can get past any barrier you could think to set up, most of the time. Though I usually don't because that would be uncivilized." She glared tellingly towards the man on the bed, who for some reason had gone eerily still at her declaration.

"And I have some questions of my own, *Zander Sariel.*" She pulled his full name from his mind with ease. "Why I woke up naked in a bed with you might be a good place to start." She shook the bag and closed the door behind her, suddenly deciding she'd rather be dressed before she had this conversation.

Regina dropped the blanket, turned on the shower and tried to block her thoughts as best she could, desperately needing a solitary moment to pull herself together. *Zander.*

She actually felt his understanding before he slipped away, leaving her completely alone with her thoughts. His absence didn't bring the immediate sense of relief and relaxation she usually got when she had her mind all to herself. That fact alone scared her out of her wits.

Who was that man? Legends of the mesmerizing attraction of the Truebloods were obviously not exaggerated. How else could she explain the way she'd responded to him?

A perfect stranger. A stranger with the ability to sense her thoughts.

Truebloods weren't supposed to be telepathic. She thought about her reaction to that bit of information. How was it that she was more irritated than petrified by his instant access to her mind? And why had she been so quick to share the truth of the abilities she had been taught for so long to hide? Especially after her recent experience with that maniac Shadow, Grey Wolf.

Her body froze beneath the spray as she took a quick mental inventory. He wasn't there. The monster who'd used his magick to tag and torture her was no longer a slithering presence in her mind or body.

She opened the shower door and glanced over her shoulder at the swiftly fogging mirror above the sink. The markings he'd so enjoyed burning into her were gone. Signs of infection had all but disappeared, and the bruises had vanished. They'd healed her. But how?

She'd been so sure it was irreversible. At least for anyone but a Shadow. That's what he'd told her. What he'd been counting on. Why Grey had been so certain she would give in.

An image flashed before her eyes of her lying on the bed, wracked with illness as she drank from Zander's arm. She knew she'd pulled it from Lux's memory. He'd risked his life for her? An Unborn? A stranger? It didn't make any sense. Not with all the horror stories she'd heard from the others.

Truebloods were cruel and judgmental. They hated Unborns. Didn't they? A wave of worry and comfort came from the other room. So, Zander hadn't disappeared completely. He was still mentally connected, hovering around the edges of her thoughts. She didn't want to dwell on why that made her feel better.

She finished washing and wrapped the towel around her long, dark hair as she rummaged through the bag of clothes. Along with several lovely peasant-style blouses like the one she'd been wearing when she arrived, she found a multitude of flowing skirts in bright jeweled tones.

The thoughtfulness and knowledge inherent in the gifts made her smile. Lux had exquisite taste. They were perfect for her. And for the current situation. She *had* returned to England, not far from where she'd been changed from a simple Gypsy girl into an Unborn Vampire, over two hundred years before. She'd returned to where it began for the end. There was a kind of poetry in that.

Sensing Zander attempting to pursue that train of thought, she proceeded to throw up block after block until he gave up and retreated in frustration. She'd have to remember how nosy he was. At least until she figured out how to effectively block him completely from her more private thoughts.

She dressed and braided her hair loosely, digging through the bag until she realized with a sigh why a man should never be allowed to go clothes shopping. Lux had forgotten to purchase underwear.

One final look in the mirror had her grimacing. She wasn't going to win any Vamp of the Universe contests, that was certain. Her face still looked drawn and ashen. She touched the tendrils of silver framing her face, a reminder of the dark evil that had nearly killed her. A chuckle escaped before she could stop it. It reminded her of one of those animated movies her fellow clan member Cooper was obsessed with. Cruella De Vil, anyone?

She tilted her head to look at it from every angle. After two hundred and eighteen years on the planet, did she finally look a teensy bit older? Some people might dream of looking eighteen forever, but for her the reality of this particular aging process was more of a burden and an irritant than a boon.

When she came out, she found Lux seated comfortably on a large leather recliner in front of the fire. She instinctively reached out with her senses until she "felt" Zander using the shower in another room. Relaxing, she gave herself a moment to take stock of her surroundings.

It was a lavish loft-style apartment above the pub. Once again she was amazed by how deceptively plain and small the outside of the building had appeared. The loft had high, beamed ceilings, and beneath several intricate, richly toned throw rugs, she saw grey stone tile on the floor.

Lux sat before a small but beautiful fireplace in one corner of the room. A long leather sofa and recliner framed the hearth, along with an antique table, sadly cluttered with keys, mail and an empty bag of potato chips.

She took in the man's elegant appearance as he lounged there, lost in thought. Deep burgundy hair caught the light of the fire and threw parts of his face in shadow. She could see a small resemblance to his brother Zander. His eyes, his smile. But where Zander was large and intimidatingly broad, Lux had the lean-muscled look of a predator. Where Zander's face was harsh and his demeanor powerful, Lux was all things beautiful and sensual.

She had a feeling his looks were deceiving—that he could be just as dangerous as his elder brother when the occasion warranted. More so. She turned to study the rest of the room.

The bed against the far wall was sumptuous and decadent. It sat on an elevated, stepped frame of dark polished wood. She could personally attest to the comfort of the king-size mattress, and the warm, soft texture of the ruby chenille throw that had covered her, which she folded and walked over to place on the edge of the bed.

She touched the deep blue comforter. It was almost the same sapphire color as Zander's eyes. Thick and soft as a cloud. It was a bed made for sex. The bed of a pasha. Or a seriously hunky Vampire.

On the other side of the room she saw a small kitchenette, one large dirty dish lying lonely in the sink, attesting to its single occupant. A seriously hunky, *bachelor* Vampire.

Her stomach chose that moment to rumble. And not for blood.

She always found it amusing to read the lore humans wrote about her kind. They weren't dead. Far from it. If anything, their "affliction" made them *more* alive than most.

From what Elizabeth had told her, several of their own scholars had long since established that vampirism, at least in the case of Truebloods, was nothing more than a variant evolution of sapiens. One of Mother Nature's many attempts at creating life, one that hadn't gone the way of the dinosaur or Neanderthal.

Madame Nicolette had a more spiritual explanation, something about a Mother goddess and guardians. It had always sounded similar to a story her Daj used to tell her as a child, though Nicolette had never fully explained it to Reggie. But both women had readily agreed that humans tended to fear and demonize things they couldn't or wouldn't understand.

The truth was that the lifespans of the Vampire extended to

thousands of years instead of a mere handful of decades. The body worked harder and rejuvenated faster than normal. Cell tissue regenerated at a swifter rate. Yes, blood was necessary to live, to replenish the busy organs, but so was the occasional meal.

She couldn't help but be happy about that particular busted myth. She wasn't sure she could have survived hundreds of years without her favorite staples—chocolate and more chocolate.

There were also those "myths" that were true for Unborns but not for Truebloods—like daylight. From her admittedly limited understanding, since she'd just met her first two this morning, natural-born Vampires could be out in the sunlight.

The older they became the easier it was. It hurt their eyes and they burned at a painfully rapid rate, but they could use strong sunscreen and dark glasses and go to the beach if they were determined to do so.

An Unborn on the other hand would die instantly, proving that most but not *all* of the genetic traits were transferred during the change. That truism had always been the hardest for Reggie to swallow. Even after all this time, she still missed the sun.

Her stomach growled again, this time so loudly that Lux looked up from his quiet contemplation with a smile. "Hungry?"

Her nod was emphatic. "I've barely eaten in weeks. It must be a sign that I'm getting better. I feel hungry enough to put a serious dent in a whole herd of cattle. Or at least a few cheeseburgers."

She walked closer to the softly chuckling Lux and put her hand on his shoulder. "Thank you for everything you've done. Taking me in, healing me. You're everything Elizabeth said you were and more."

Lux stood and took her hand in his own. His eyes, so like his brother's, seemed to twinkle with a warmth that drew her even closer as he spoke. "So are you, Reggie."

At her surprised look he continued. "Lizzy still keeps in contact with me every now and then. When we figured out your name last night, I realized I was in the presence of the sweet, young Gypsy with amazing abilities that she is always bragging about."

Reggie looked down in shy denial, secretly pleased that Elizabeth had spoken so highly of her, only to jump when he let go of her hand to lift up one side of her blouse. "I need to check your wound." His tone was very matter of fact. "I have a salve that will speed the healing process. The site was badly infected."

He took a small vial from his pocket, opened the top and proceeded to spread the thick gel-like substance over the tender area on her lower back. His broad fingers were gentle, but she still flinched at the cool feel of the mixture as it absorbed into her heated skin.

"You'll have to take it easy for another day, and you'll need more blood from Zander." Her whole body stiffened in rejection at the thought.

He looked up from applying the salve to the injury and caught her worried gaze. A momentary twinge of guilt flashed from his mind to hers before he sighed, drawing her attention to his words.

"Reggie, you could no doubt heal completely with an extensive amount of rest, some protein and a regular dose of synthetic blood. The dark magick has been purged, but your natural immunities and self-healing abilities are still a bit too sluggish for my liking. That means it might take *days* for you to mend. Perhaps a week or more. *Unless* you receive more blood from Zander." Lux winked at her devilishly, attempting to calm her fears. "Or me."

"Lux, you're my brother and I love you. But you're enjoying rubbing that gunk on my woman a little bit *too* much. And since there's no way Regina is taking anything you're offering, apart from your skills as a healer, let's all just sit down and make sure your *patient* is well-fed."

Reggie looked up with a glower while Lux raised his hands and took a big, dramatic step back. She fumed at Zander as he stood in the doorway, freshly showered, a tight smile on his face and a large platter of something that smelled delicious in his hands.

He returned her angry gaze for a moment, before stepping over to the small kitchen to divvy up the food and gather silverware, utterly ignoring her pique.

"You are so lucky I'm hungry. If I wasn't, I might tell you that no one calls me Regina. My name is Reggie. I might also tell you that I have never been, nor am I planning to be, anyone's woman. And who I allow to touch me is *my* choice, not yours."

Lux led her silently towards the sofa as Zander set her plate down on the coffee table. She plopped down and crossed her arms, using all her willpower to hold her pose, determined not to dive headfirst into the scrumptious-looking feast in front of her.

Lux took the recliner and Zander sat on the couch beside Reggie. *Right* beside her, his hip pressing against hers. When she tried to scoot over, he placed an arm around her shoulders, effectively trapping her against his side.

He speared a small, spiced potato with his fork and held it to her mouth, his expression determined. She couldn't resist the temptation. He waited until she was chewing ecstatically before he spoke.

"You don't know me very well yet, so I understand that you may be under the assumption that I don't say exactly what I mean."

He shoved another potato into her mouth. "I am also a little possessive and I apologize now if that upsets you, but I'm far too old and set in my ways to change."

A piece of tenderloin that practically melted in her mouth was next. "And the fact that no one else calls you Regina, while a shame because it's a glorious name and it suits you, only makes me that much more determined to do so." He used the hand cradling her shoulder to push a stray strand of hair out of her wary eyes, and continued to feed her.

Her confusion and discomfort must have shown on her face, because Lux quickly chimed in, making a quick face at his brother before moving closer to the edge of the recliner. His food sat forgotten on the table as he caught her eye with a gentle smile.

"Now that you're feeling better, I think its time for you to tell us why you requested sanctuary. And why did Lizzy send you out alone? She knows all she has to do is contact me and I'd help her anyway I could."

Reggie felt Zander trying to burrow into her mind again, and she stood before turning on him. "Okay, I don't know how you can do that, but you need to stop right now!"

She watched as Lux raised his eyebrows at Zander until he shrugged in apology. He sent a sheepish glance towards Reggie before taking her hand to pull her back down beside him.

"I'm sorry for invading your privacy, Regina. I'm not known for my subtlety."

Lux covered his mouth in an apparent coughing fit that earned a warning glare from Zander. He turned to Reggie once more. "If it makes you feel any better, you're already getting much better at blocking me, which you shouldn't be able to do in the first place. And I don't like it one little bit."

The last made Reggie smile. It did make her feel better. She was used to doing the snooping, but this last month had taught her that being on the other end of such an invasion made you feel powerless and violated.

She realized the two men were looking at her expectantly, and she knew that the time had come to tell them the story. Well, most of it.

"Elizabeth didn't tell you because she didn't know I was coming. I blocked her after she tried to contact me the last time. No one at the Deva castle knows where I am. And that's how I want it to stay." Her words seemed to disturb them.

"You can block your sire?" The two men spoke in near-simultaneous amazement. She knew they found it hard to believe. It wasn't supposed to be possible. She hadn't even been aware she could do it until the night of her capture.

All she'd known was that she would rather die than lead Elizabeth and the others into that animal's clutches, and she'd visualized a wall, the kind she'd seen in the minds of so many others, a wall that her protective friend and creator could not scale.

When no one had come to save her, she knew she'd been successful. She'd been trapped until the Shadow had let down his guard enough to allow her the chance to escape.

Zander ran a hand through his hair and looked towards his brother. "How is this possible? How can she block her sire?" He turned to Reggie. "You say you're a Reader. I've touched your thoughts, I know you have the ability to sense what others are thinking, but just how far does that ability go?"

Reggie hesitated, not sure where to start, or even how much to say, but Lux saved her from making an attempt as he

39

began to speak, his voice solemn. "As a species, along with longevity, healing and a few other unique abilities, Vampires have always had the ability to *feel* the presence of another of our own, as well as that of the Weres." Zander nodded quickly, as if urging him on.

"We also have the ability to control or manipulate the minds of those humans and Weres whose blood we share. Although—" He held up his hand as Zander opened his mouth to interrupt. "Glynn once told me that all Vampires at one time had extraordinary telepathic abilities. But over several generations of politics and suspicion and obsession with *lineage,*" Lux emphasized the word with obvious distaste, "we simply forgot. Now, apart from the three known exceptions, we've all but lost our gifts."

"*Three* exceptions?" Reggie looked at both the brothers in question. Liz had only told her about the sire-child connection.

Lux nodded. "Yes. The sire, both natural mother of a Trueblood and the creator of an Unborn, will share a mental line with their children. It's a protective measure that never went away. Call it our version of the maternal instinct.

Secondly, there are the Healers such as Glynn Magriel, and those who train under her." He placed a hand on his chest. "We spend years studying control of the mind, the use of certain herbs, tonics and techniques on unlocking our existing but dormant abilities—to help those who are in need of care. The patient has to be agreeable, however, for their natural guard to fall enough to allow us to sense and attempt to manage their pain. Even then, it's more of a feeling than an actual clear-cut communication."

"And the third?"

Lux and Zander both looked away from her for a moment, and her eyes narrowed at their hesitation. This time it was

Zander who answered, in a voice tinged with deep satisfaction. "The third exception is when a Vampire finds and shares blood with his *grathita*. His mate. The bond there is stronger than mere telepathy. It is a complete merging of souls. We call it Unity."

Reggie's eyes grew large as she realized that she had heard that word before. *Grathita*. When they were kissing he had mentally called her his...she shook her head. She must have been mistaken. She swallowed a little nervously and looked over the table to find Lux eyeing her with intense interest. "So...only those three then?"

Lux nodded. "With the new and interesting exception of one fairly young Unborn Reader."

He raised his brow, waiting for the knowledge to sink in. "You, dear Reggie, are an anomaly. In fact, according to the Clan Trust you shouldn't exist. The rules banning Unborn creation are fairly recent in our species' history. But the rules against turning Readers? Those have been around since the inception of the Trust."

She shifted uncomfortably as they continued to stare at her in silence. Lux appeared fascinated by her existence. Zander, however, had such a grim expression on his face that she had to look away.

She knew she was an anomaly. Liz had told her as much several times over the years. She'd been warned not to share her unique abilities with anyone outside of the family. So she'd always stayed close to home, only using her gifts in the defense of her clan.

It wasn't a hardship. She'd had never been a particularly good fighter, and all of the other abilities that appeared to come so naturally to the others, shape-shifting in particular, always seemed to elude her.

Instead, she'd been assigned to semi-permanent recon duty. Reggie was a spy. Which is how she'd gotten into this mess in the first place.

Zander tugged her onto his lap in reaction to her distress. She was too caught up in memories to fight him, but her inner voice reminded her to take him to task on his domineering behavior at the next opportunity.

She began to tell them about her last assignment. It had seemed so simple and straightforward at the time. She'd been sent by Madame Nicolette, the clan mother and cofounder of their rag-tag family, to spy on Arygon Dydarren and his pack of hoodlum Weres.

Lux nodded and she assumed Liz must have told him all about the pack of Werewolves whose territory bordered theirs near Lago Maggiore. Since long before Reggie had joined the family, Arygon had been pestering the predominantly female members of the Deva Clan over one imagined slight or another.

The last several decades they'd had a few minor scuffles, mostly over Arygon's assertion that Hannah, her clan's most recent addition, had killed the Were's brother Jasyn Dydarren. It was of course, completely untrue.

Jasyn and the Roaring-Twenties flapper had been lovers before she'd been changed. What happened between them was not Reggie's story to tell, and she'd respected Hannah's privacy. Even when her friend's silent grief threatened to overwhelm the sensitive telepath. Reggie could only hope that Jasyn would someday return from wherever it was he'd disappeared to.

She lost herself in the memories as she thought back to three months before, when the Were attacks had picked up and strange things started occurring in the nearby village.

One night, while the clan members had spread out to aid in the search for a young boy who'd gone missing, Hannah had been separated from the party. She was tricked by what she'd described as a horrible illusion. Badly injured, her heart was nearly pulled from her body before she'd managed to escape.

Both Nicolette and Liz had been beside themselves with rage until they knew Hannah would survive. When cooler heads had prevailed, Madame had called Reggie in and asked her to go to the pack's den and try to find out why the attacks had picked up in both skill and violence.

Nicolette had been more than baffled at the pack's actions. And she seemed positive that Arygon didn't have the ability, or the desire for that matter, to plan such odious maneuvers. She'd been right.

Arygon had always been arrogant, it was his defining characteristic. So his decision to form an alliance with another pack was completely unexpected. Apparently, his ego had been set aside to placate his all-consuming need for vengeance against the Devas.

He had offered his fealty to the representative of a powerful and ancient group of fringe Weres. Weres that were supposed to be long dead. Creatures that practiced the dark arts with terrifying skill, not content with the natural earth magick of the lupine breed. Werewolves that had no real care for rules or binding laws or oaths, too busy lusting after blood and power.

Les Loups De L'Ombre. The Shadow Wolves.

She had heard stories about these villains on her Daj Mia's knee. The Gypsies had always believed such creatures existed, but she'd never before thought to see one. And she'd certainly never expected to be the focus of one's undivided and sadistic attentions.

When she'd seen Arygon kneel before the darkly handsome man, she had known what he was. He wore his malevolent power like a black shroud. It covered him even as it reached out to envelop those around him.

She had been safely hidden behind a tree, her position masking her scent as the young men of Dydarren's Pack dressed in ceremonial robes and gathered in the wood to solidify the unholy allegiance.

Reggie could sense Arygon's fear and hesitation and wondered what on earth he could have been thinking. Didn't he know the stories? Didn't he know that he was ending his family's long and, for the most part, peaceful reign with this single damning action?

"You have seen but a taste of what I can do, what you can accomplish if you ally with *Les Loups De L'Ombre*, young Arygon. You may not have the taste for blood needed to get the results you desire. That is why *I* am here—why this alliance would be so beneficial to you." The insidious voice pierced her skin and caused her to shiver in fear.

"Will you join with us willingly this night, that your enemies shall become our enemies, their departure or demise our only concern, their end our goal?" His hypnotic tone wove around Arygon's prostrate form. The words a fulfillment of his darkest wish...the end of the Deva Clan. He nodded and lifted his hands as if in supplication.

"Grey Wolf, Shaman and Warrior of the Shadow, I willingly join my pack with yours. I offer all that we are and accept your aid in the removal of my enemies. *Our* enemies."

With the formal words spoken, the men that filled the clearing dropped their robes and howled towards the moon, their bodies overtaken by transformation. Reggie watched in fascination as their shimmering forms stretched and cracked, taking the shape of their nightmarish counterparts.

Standing as men around the roaring flames of the bonfire, were the true beasts of legend. The Werewolf. Their muzzles grotesquely elongated, their large forms covered in fur, curving claws glinting in the dancing light.

She could see the beauty and freedom inherent in the primitive change, as they allowed their inner beings escape from within the limited human shell. She felt them all reveling in the release. Except for one.

Grey, the dark leader, had yet to change. He looked at Arygon's men with a patient, even encouraging smile, but she could feel his disgust, his distaste for all of them. She almost felt sorry for Arygon. Or she would have if he hadn't sold his soul for the chance to kill off her family.

She was just about to leave, to share what she'd learned with the others, when she'd heard it. A bloodcurdling scream. She reached out with her gifts and knew before the tiny form was dragged into the clearing who it would be.

Young Maria, the shop owner's daughter from the village. Reggie knew her well. Her father had always been a good and loyal friend of her clan.

She sensed Grey Wolf's twisted leap of excitement, and realized in a heartbeat not only what had happened to the small boy who'd gone missing just a few nights before, but what was about to happen to this young, innocent human if she didn't find a way to stop it.

Too far away from the castle and unwilling to put any more of her clan at risk, she had to think fast. There was no way she could fight her way through this large group of male wolves successfully.

She could barely hold her own in one-to-one combat. She would have to use the only skills she possessed, and hope to confuse them enough to allow Maria the opportunity to escape. She had to do something. She could not let an innocent be sacrificed right before her eyes.

"Why waste your sacrifice on a mere human, when you could seal the deal with an enemy instead?" She spoke directly into their minds, purposely making them hear her voice all around the clearing, so that they couldn't tell where she was actually hiding.

Arygon leapt up and his followers went wild, banging the brush, trying to find the spy in their midst. Grey tilted his head and closed his eyes, eerily still amongst the chaos.

"Come on, fellas. If you're going to go against the rules Arygon's father and his father before him put in place, break blood vows and actually set out to harm a member of the village you're all sworn to protect, surely you'd have no problem finding a harmless little vamp like me. A *girl* no less."

Some of the Weres had paused in their search to listen to her words, hearing truth in the condemnation. Arygon, as well, seemed to feel the bite of shame, shifting back to his human form.

She took heart. Maybe she could get through to them after all. Maybe she could fight against the Shadow Wolf's tempting offer by reminding them that, while the Devas and the Dydarren Pack may hate each other now, they had always agreed that their human neighbors were not to be harmed.

The Unborn Vampires took blood from the willing, and only what was needed. The Werewolves were masters of the hunt, sharing any excess with the town for a reasonable fee. The sacrifice of young virgins had never been a part of the deal.

"Your offer is generous. We accept." She heard his voice behind her just before an arm wrapped around her throat, dragging her from her hiding place and towards the fire.

She dangled in the air, her legs flailing and her heart racing with fear. He shouldn't have been able to find her. She hadn't even noticed him move. She had a feeling she had seriously misjudged the situation.

"Let Maria go."

Grey Wolf tightened his arm around her neck, nearly cutting off her air supply. He chuckled in her ear, nuzzling her hair as he wrapped his other arm around her waist. "Gladly, my beauty, gladly."

He made a gesture and the Were who had been restraining the young, sobbing girl opened his arms.

Maria looked fearfully towards Reggie, before turning and racing through the trees faster than she'd ever moved in her short life. Reggie's body relaxed in relief for a moment, until Grey whipped her around to face him, wrenching her arms behind her back.

"Who have we here?" He studied her features intently, taking special note of the mark on her forehead, the mark Daj Mia had bestowed upon her when she'd turned sixteen and gained control of her abilities.

Arygon took a step forward, animosity and something else, quickly hidden, in his expression. "Her?"

He scoffed. "She's no one. A nothing little Gypsy with delusions of grandeur. She's the weakest of the lot—the others do all her fighting for her. What happened, little Reggie? Did you get lost in the woods? Where are your protectors?"

She kept her expression blank. She knew what they thought of her. Let them underestimate her. While they did, she was busy sneaking around in their thoughts, trying to find a way out of her current mess.

When she reached into his mind, she was oddly touched to find that Arygon had a desire to let her go. It wasn't her he hated. Wasn't her he was after. He hadn't even thought beyond punishing the Deva Clan for the wrongs they'd done him. Now he was wondering how he could get her away to safety.

But that didn't make sense. Didn't Arygon want to kill all of them? Isn't that why he'd made this deal with the devil?

The hands on her arms tightened, causing her to tense in pain. Grey was a bit harder to read. "I don't think your pretty Gypsy is as helpless as she would like us to believe. Was it weakness that had you pups chasing your tails a moment ago? Is it weakness that has her even now poking through our minds, searching for a weapon to use against us? I don't think so. I'd call it power. And I'd be willing to bet our little beauty has it in spades."

Grey sniffed her neck and smiled, the first genuine smile of delight she'd seen, and on him the expression terrified her.

"So much power in such a tiny thing. *Too* much. And you don't appreciate it at all do you? You don't even know what you have. Such a shame."

He leaned in to whisper in her ear, his voice laced with some dark undercurrent that she hoped she was imagining. "I can teach you how to use it. I can teach you things you never even imagined. With me, you can be more than the bloodsuckers' little snoop. With me, you can be a queen. As you were destined to be."

She blanched and her lips curled in disgust as she saw what dwelt within his mind. A nightmare of perversion and cruelty, pain and domination. And his plans for her were anything but selfless. She looked up into his fever bright eyes and sneered mockingly in answer.

He laughed, not at all the response Reggie had been expecting, and threw her into a nearby Were's open arms.

"Prepare her for me. Make sure the rope is strong."

Reggie blinked as if awakening from a fog to find Lux kneeling before her, a concerned frown on his face.

Zander was holding her so tightly she was worried she might lose circulation, his expression one of quiet rage. She immediately brought down every mental barrier she had, realizing the visions and emotions she'd been reliving had probably spilled over to him without her knowing. He'd already seen more than she would have liked.

She stammered a little as she told them all that she'd learned of Grey's plans while he'd held her prisoner, but she couldn't stem the tide of fear and helplessness those memories induced.

Zander only held her tighter, pressing her head into his neck, as if he could absorb her pain and take it into himself. It was almost too tempting to take the comfort he offered. She pushed gently against his chest and stood, moving behind the couch with a shrug.

"That's pretty much it. I managed to escape, injured but alive. I sent out a message to Elizabeth, to warn the clan about Grey Wolf and his plans...and then I ran. After I saw what was in his head, what he and those he was gathering had planned not just for us, but for the entire species, I knew the only way to stop them was to come here and ask for sanctuary from the Truebloods. To ask for help."

They looked at her incredulously. She knew they wanted to hear it all. What she'd been forced to endure at Grey Wolf's hands, how she'd gotten him to relax his guard enough for her to escape. But there were some things she wasn't sure she'd ever be able to share. Some things she wished to forget.

She shakily stood her ground, though she could feel fatigue weighing her down, her body temperature cooling with a dramatic swiftness. The memories had taken their toll, and she was still weak.

"Okay, no more questions for now, Reggie. But you do need

blood."

"I'm fine, really." She knew what Lux was leading up to.

"I feel great. I think that first dose helped a lot more than you thought it would. Besides, I was planning on heading out in a little while anyway, to pick up a few necessaries. I could grab a quick drink while I'm gone." She moved around the couch and headed towards the door.

"Lux."

She glanced over at Zander, sitting quietly on the couch, and shivered at the determined gleam in his eye.

"Yes, Zander?"

"I need some time alone with Regina." Authority filled his tone.

Lux didn't hesitate. He rose rapidly and pointed to the kitchen on his way out the door. "The rest of the salve and tonic are on the counter, though I doubt you'll need it. And I'll be right downstairs badgering the bartender if you need me." Then he was gone.

Reggie turned to watch the door shut solidly behind him, leaving her alone. She peeked over her shoulder at the silent man on the couch.

Well, not exactly alone. Alone with *Zander*. And that was the problem.

Chapter Three

Zander attempted to calm his racing pulse, to ease the temper and desire fighting for supremacy within him. She looked as if she might bolt at any moment, had even taken several steps towards the door that Lux had so recently closed. She seemed so pale and fragile in that moment that it nearly weakened his resolve.

He reached out with his newly awakened senses and he could hear all the thoughts racing in her head. It was like the flutter of wings in his mind, he couldn't make out exactly what she was thinking, but the basic gist was clear.

She wanted him, but she was afraid of her feelings. More than that, she was afraid of what sharing blood with him once more would do. She was clever, and she had a very strong feeling that his ability to sense her thoughts was connected with the sharing session of the night before. After their earlier conversation, it wouldn't take her long to acknowledge the truth she was dancing around so hesitantly. That she belonged to him.

His thoughts weren't nearly so complicated. This woman, whether she knew it or not, had just thrown down the gauntlet.

First, by withholding information of her capture when he knew there was more to her story. He could feel it. A part of him was thankful, the rage already coursing through his veins at what she'd revealed was almost more than he could bear.

The Trueblood Mediator, for the first time in his sensible and centered life, wanted to kill. *Not* quickly. He wanted to tear Grey Wolf apart piece by painful piece.

If the secrets she'd kept weren't enough to send his temper to the very edge, she'd had the audacity to not only refuse her mate's blood, but to imply that she would take from another.

She would actually prefer placing herself in danger by leaving Haven just to avoid being close to him? She had to know he'd never let her.

He realized she didn't yet comprehend the true nature of what was happening between them. Few Unborns knew of the Unity between natural Vampires and their mates.

Reggie's sire had been wed to one, but they hadn't been truly mated. Malcolm had confided in him often during that time. Zander knew his connection to Elizabeth had been a loyal and loving one, but it had never been the *grathita saha asan*, truly bound together in the blood.

Her trembling increased and he pushed back his possessive jealousy to focus on her. She needed blood if she was to grow strong. And his was the only sustenance she'd ever have again. Such was the way of their kind. He was about to give his Regina a lesson she'd never forget.

He let his resolve and desire wrap around her just moments before he stood and began to walk slowly in her direction. Her eyes grew wide, and her lips parted on soft, panting breaths. His lustful thoughts hit their mark, filling her mind with erotic images of his plans.

"Yes, Regina mine. Feel how I need you."

She took another, subtle step back, still attempting to resist his pull, but it was obvious she was waging a losing battle.

He knew the moment she recalled the feel of his lips on hers, his weight pressing her into the mattress, the exact instant she decided to give in to her own desire. His fists tightened in triumph when he realized she'd stopped fighting. She wanted more...and he wanted everything.

Each brush of his tailored pants against his cock was a torment. Every step an agony of pleasure as he thought of all the things he wanted to do to her.

He caught a stray thought in the fragile mental pathway their first blood-sharing had created. It was a thought she'd had before. Incomplete, and yet it chilled him.

They had healed her, given her sanctuary. He knew he would slay any Trust member or renegade Shadow Wolf who dared to threaten his *grathita* now that he'd found her. So what was going through her labyrinthine mind? What was this grand plan?

And why was she still so sure she was going to die?

Zander stopped in front of her and leaned down until his lips were a breath away from her own. "One of these days you're going to tell me about this secret plan of yours and why it worries me so damn much." He lifted her easily in his arms, his hands cradling her spread thighs as she wrapped her legs around his waist.

"But not right now." He walked her towards his luxurious bed. "Right now you're going to feed, and then I'm going to do what I've been dying to do from the moment I saw you dancing in my pub." He set her gently down in the middle of the bedspread, its dark blue color the perfect foil for her raven hair and creamy skin.

He needed to be inside her more than he needed his next breath. The sight of her, eyes soft, body open and waiting for him, was almost his undoing. The fact that she'd recently been so close to death was the only thing that held him back long enough to ensure she got what she needed first. Blood.

He'd replenished himself with some of the synthesized blood Lux kept in the refrigerator in his room for emergencies. He'd known she'd have need of him again and for some reason, heading downstairs to drink from a willing volunteer hadn't tempted him in the least. All he wanted was to return to Regina. She was the only ambrosia he craved.

He stood above her and began to unbutton his shirt, giving himself a moment to rein in his need for her.

Reggie pushed herself up on her elbows, flinging that obstinate strand of hair out of her eyes before attempting a rather weak glare.

It was hard to be angry while watching him undress with a sensual skill that left her trembling, slowly revealing his impressive physique to the tune of her pounding heart. "We're going to have to work on that tone of yours first, 'Oh Great and Powerful Master'."

Zander's blue eyes flashed with a fire that sent Reggie scuttling backwards on the bed. She got a sudden image of herself through his eyes. Naked, hands tied to the headboard with silken scarves, completely at his mercy.

"Oh no you don't." She gasped, even as the vision caused her body to tense with lust, showing its readiness with a flood of arousal that had her pressing her thighs together in shock. After all she'd been through how could she even consider trusting him that much?

The lust on his face dimmed for a moment, before he quickly finished shedding his clothes to join her on the bed. He took her chin in one hand, gently unraveling her braid with the other.

"Don't compare us to that, Regina. I would never do anything to hurt you. All I want, all I'll ever want, is your happiness and pleasure." His eyes went dark as he spread her dark hair over her shoulders.

His broad fingers caressed her silky blouse, and she resented for a moment the fabric that separated her from his touch. No sooner had the thought formed than a zap of electricity shot through her body, followed by a sudden chill, before she realized with a gasp that she was completely naked, her clothes nowhere to be found.

He tapped her nose and his eyes sparkled with mischief. "Being a Trueblood comes with a few special...perks."

A chuckle gurgled up from her chest, astonishing her with its joyous sound. She shrugged and wrapped her arms around his broad shoulders, kissing his jaw while he looked down at her as if staggered by her easy acceptance.

She snuck a peek at him before sighing dramatically. "Impressive. Now if only Super Vampire would use his powers for good."

Zander's mouth quirked, dimples deepening before, in a swift and surprising move, she found herself sitting on top of his thighs as he lay beneath her on the bed, his hands light on her hips, careful of her tender wound.

"I'll show you just how good I can be." He promised. "*After* you drink."

She was having a hard time following his directive. The view was just far too captivating to be ignored. He was so big, so male, and so...delicious-looking. Zander looked at her from beneath his thick lashes with a knowing grin.

"*Then taste me.*"

His deep voice echoed in her head, lips unmoving. She really needed to figure out how he was doing that. But not now.

Now she would do what he asked. In her own way, of course. She just couldn't resist.

Pulling her long hair over one shoulder, she leaned down to kiss and nip at his taut abs. They tensed beneath her lips and she smiled, feeling his excitement, his desire without him needing to say a word. She worked her way up, teasing him in the same way she knew he'd meant to tease her earlier, sucking his hardening nipples into her mouth until he struggled for breath.

She leaned forward and licked his lips, staying just out of reach before lowering her mouth once more, bypassing his offered neck in favor of heading further down towards his impressive erection.

He was beautiful. Long and thick and hard, the silken tip already dripping with his desire...for *her*. She felt her womb clench at the thought of how he would fill her. She softly kissed the darkening head of his shaft, before lapping gently with her tongue, gathering the sinful, salty taste of him in her mouth.

His hips jerked upward instinctively at the sensation, his hands gathering in her hair before she could take him fully into her mouth.

"Not yet, Regina."

Zander released her hair to grasp her under her arms and drag her up his body, a moan of mutual need escaping at the friction they created. He wrapped one firm hand around the back of her neck and lifted his chin, offering himself to her. "Drink."

His command shivered through her, drew all her attention to the blood pulsing strongly through the vein in his neck. She could feel the reins he held on his desire, how much he needed her to taste him.

Through his memories she relived her unconscious feeding

of the night before. The sensations that had burned through him at the touch of her lips, the feel of her fangs sinking into his flesh. He wanted her, *needed* her.

She moaned, leaning forward, rubbing her wetness against his pulsing cock, laving his neck with her tongue. Her fangs extending, breaking through her gums before piercing his skin.

The warm, thick liquid touched her tongue and her heart sang. Here was that feeling she had sensed from him. *Yes...* It was a pleasure unlike any she had known.

Her thirsty cells drank him in, absorbed him, one with all that he was. She was home.

Her body was healing, the aches disappearing. He gave her his strength without reservation. And then there was the need. It increased until she was mad with it, her body readying itself for this man. Zander. She needed him inside her, needed him filling her body as he was already filling her soul.

He groaned against her mouth, the sound vibrating on her lips and she answered in kind. He rolled her beneath him, careful not to break contact or jar her with his movements.

"I can't wait." She heard his thought a moment before he raised her legs high and entered her with one slow, powerful thrust.

She released him with a sharp cry of need as he filled her. Licking his throat instinctively to help close the wound before arching beneath him, she silently begged for more.

She felt him stretching her, her muscles tightening around him in instinctive rejection when he pulled back before sinking deep once more.

He leaned forward and sucked her nipple hard against the roof of his mouth, releasing it to lick gently, his breath against her skin causing it to tighten to a hard peak. He repeated the process—again and again he ate at her breasts, the movement of his hips against her slow and torturous as he sampled her flesh.

"*So tight around me. So wet, Regina. It feels so good, my love.*"

She heard him in her mind, watched him gorge on her breasts, his eyes closed in mindless delight, full mouth tilted in rapture.

He angled her pelvis higher, his rigid arousal hitting that magical bundle of secret nerves that had her wavering on the brink of something amazing.

The blood in her veins began to heat, her limbs quivering as he thrust inside her. In moments she was falling over the edge, the deliciously sweet taste of him still hot on her tongue. Her muscles rippled, contracting around him and he growled against her flesh.

He pulled out quickly, sinking down on the bed, his mouth replacing one source of nourishment with another. "Zander!" She moaned aloud, her hands moving to clench in his golden hair. His tongue lightly flicked her clit before lowering to lap at her flowing juices.

"*Manna. Manna from heaven. So sweet on my tongue. I want more.*"

His intimate words had her arching against his face as he nuzzled her dark curls with his nose. His tongue slid inside her damp entrance, thrusting lightly, teasingly, curling the tip to gather more of her flavor. Lips wrapped around her swollen bud, pulling it into his mouth to suckle with gentle pressure.

"*There?*"

"Yes. Yes, there."

In moments, she found herself soaring again, before she'd even had a chance to catch her breath. Her muscles trembled and her blood rushed loud in her ears as she called out his name, "Zander."

And still it wasn't enough. She needed him inside her, needed to feel his release more than she craved her own. The feeling was so strong she must have projected it outward. He growled his agreement, lifting himself from the feast between her thighs to enter her once more.

Zander's eyes blazed down into her own. Both wordlessly acknowledged the exquisite feel of his cock buried deep within her, the intensity of the moment.

He swooped down to take her mouth with a desperation that thrilled her. The taste of her own juices on his tongue. When she licked the sheen of her arousal from his lips, his eyes darkened to a deep midnight blue. He smiled down at her, his extended fangs gleaming, thrusts increasing.

"Yes. Taste how delicious you are. Feel what you do to me, priya, *my beloved."*

Never had she felt so full, so stretched, so...taken. Each powerful stroke of his cock inside her marked her, changed her, pushed her closer to an ecstasy unlike any she'd ever known.

Her eyes snagged on where their bodies were joined, his thick width spreading her open, her arousal coating his length, easing his way.

She looked up to find him watching her, his face flushed with restrained desire, his jaw clenched in need.

Sliding his broad palm between her shoulder blades, he lifted her up against him, his other hand holding them both steady as he looked into her eyes.

"As one." He sent her an image and she felt his flare of excitement. She shakily nodded her agreement. Wanting it just as much. Needing it.

He lowered his mouth to her neck, sinking his teeth into the curve of her throat while she did the same. He was thrusting faster within her, deeper—his blood sliding down her throat like liquid heaven. Suddenly, everything converged in a flash of blinding white light as they leapt off the cliff together. Merged. *Unity.*

Confusion filled her. One minute she'd been riding a blissful wave of delight, the next she'd been overwhelmed by a thousand and one sensations, only half of them her own.

She felt his cock jerk deep inside her as he came, and his own exaltation and excitement at the feeling of her inner walls massaging him. The fire shooting down her spine, and the lightning flaying his.

The dual sensations were maddening, phenomenal. It was as if they had joined more than their bodies, more than their minds. Their souls had merged, twining together in joyous recognition.

It was terrifying.

This was not the lighthearted, lust-filled romp she had envisioned. She'd tried to convince herself that she could keep her distance, enjoy the moment and still do everything she knew she must...and then this happened.

Zander Sariel. What was it about him? Why did it suddenly feel as if nothing would ever be the same? As if she would never be the same.

She licked her mark away once more and held still until he'd released her to lie beside her on the bed.

The clothing she'd been wearing before he'd zapped them away were neatly folded on the recliner by the fire, and she left the bed before he could stop her, leaping towards them as if towards a lifeline.

Her legs were still trembling from the aftershocks of the

experience. Her skin tingled as she lifted the peasant blouse and quickly pulled it over her head to hide her naked flesh.

Taking a deep breath she turned towards him, her smile wobbly. "I'd love to know how you did that." She gestured towards the skirt she was slipping over her hips. "It's probably some secret macho trick that Trueblood fathers teach their sons when they start dating."

The chuckle stuck in a throat gone dry and tight with nerves. She had to get out of here, get some perspective before she lost what little control she had left.

Zander had been lying silent on the bed, his arm covering his eyes as he caught his breath after the most amazing sex of his life. He had to focus.

His logical mind was attempting to wrest control from his more primitive instincts that were even now howling with the need to drag his woman back where she belonged. To take her again and again until she no longer had the strength to run from him, until she could do nothing but accept the truth of their union.

He hadn't wanted it to end. Tasting her as she came, feeling her wet heat embracing him, the sound of her voice when she called his name. He'd wanted it all to last forever. But as the fire raced up his spine and blood pounded hot and heavy through his near-to-bursting cock, he knew it was wishful thinking.

Never in all his years on this earth had he felt so out of control. And when he was able to blood-share with her once again, one step closer to total Unity with his *grathita*, any chance of holding back disappeared.

She was afraid. He could feel it, even through the powerful blocks she was so very good at erecting in his path. Those blocks that were even now losing their ability to deter him as the sharing brought him further into her mind.

He knew she had found pleasure in his arms unlike any she'd ever known. That wasn't what caused her to flee like a frightened rabbit from the bed they'd just shared. It was Unity.

His father had always warned him that when he found his *grathita* and experienced his first true sharing, the world as he knew it would be changed forever.

Zander had scoffed along with his brother, believing himself above the silly displays of affection his mother and father so often engaged in. Their mother had them all wrapped around her little finger, but he had been so confident that no other woman would ever hold him in such sway.

Alexander Sariel deserved one hell of an apology. But at least he'd prepared him. As prepared as anyone could be for such a personal invasion.

Blood mates were a blessing, a beautiful gift from the Mother, but it was still a difficult transition, even for a natural-born. He could only imagine how Regina, someone so young, someone who had been human only two centuries before, would be affected by the connection.

The knowledge that another shared your emotions, your feelings...your secrets.

She was edging towards the door, determined to flee. A heartbeat later he was there, taking her into his arms. "I wish you'd quit trying to run away from me. You're putting a serious dent in my ego."

He felt her laughter against his chest, her breath choppy. "I'm beginning to doubt a sledgehammer could accomplish that feat. Remember, I know practically everything about you now."

She grew still as the words slipped out of her own mouth. He knew she'd just realized what she'd admitted out loud. The very truth she'd been running from.

He held her closer, rubbing her back in understanding, even sharing a bit of her horror at the invasion of her privacy. He wouldn't change the miraculous act of their merging for the world. She was his heart, his *grathita*. But he was overwhelmed by the sadness and anger that he shared with her for what she had already experienced in her young life. The memories that rushed into him as if they were his own.

Taken from the loving arms of her grandmother at the tender age of sixteen, in order to become little more than a slave for her father and brothers, criminals all. No control, no say in what happened in her life until, at the age of eighteen, the night before she was to be sold to a horrible man so that her father could continue to drink himself into oblivion, her life had once again been dramatically altered.

He could only be grateful to Elizabeth, though he never believed he would ever use that word in the same sentence with the chit, for giving Regina the opportunity to escape her intended fate. Yet he knew that the young girl she'd been had been horrified when she finally realized what she had become.

She shifted in his arms, before speaking so softly he had to strain to hear. "They were storytellers. That's what they said when they showed up at our campsite. It was Nicolette and Elizabeth and a few of the others. They were all so very beautiful."

They'd offered to tell the lusty men in Reggie's family the greatest stories ever told, in exchange for the warmth of the fire, some food and a tent to share for the night. Her father and brothers had been overwhelmed by their good fortune. Four beautiful women for four desperate and lonely men. They'd agreed immediately.

She'd watched as the Madame stood by the fire, spinning a tale of magickal curses, Vampires and death. Her hair fell in

63

shimmering blonde waves, near silver in the moonlight, as she gestured and moved with the elegance of royalty. She was captivating.

Another woman, so different with her wild auburn locks and fiery eyes, had introduced herself as Elizabeth.

The young Gypsy had thought to herself that this was what she wanted for herself. Everything they represented. Female confidence, freedom—even the sure sensuality they wore like a second skin.

And there was something else. A power that rippled just beneath the surface of all of them. Something she couldn't define, couldn't read clearly, which should have alarmed her. But she knew they were special. She imagined that they were what she would be—if she had the freedom to choose.

Regina had fed them and listened as she finished mending one of her father's favorite shirts, the last task she would do for him before he sold her off like a prized goat to that dirty little man who'd approached them in the nearby town.

Her father had told her that she was doing far more for him in trade than she ever would by remaining. Slowing them down, taking their food and what little resources they had, holding them back from greatness.

It said a lot about the hardships of the last few years that she'd barely felt a twinge of pain at the insult. Or the hateful black thoughts he believed were secreted away in his mind, hidden from the strange, golden-eyed witch of a child who frightened him so. Just like her mother. All she felt was a profound loneliness and a wish for brighter days.

Later that night, while stoking the fire one last time before disappearing into her tiny little ragged tent, she'd heard a strange noise.

"I knew my brothers had taken the women into their tent.

That the Madame had gone over the hill with my father." Zander brushed her hair behind her ear, the already tenderly familiar gesture not lost on her as she forged through the memory.

"They had never hidden their evening 'activities' from me, despite my inexperience. I had learned not to seek them out."

But the noise had been unusual. A stifled cry of surprised pain rather than pleasure. And Reggie, concerned more for the women she had so admired than her relatives, had sought out the sound.

As she drew closer, she'd sensed her brother's horror reach out to her just moments before she poked her head quietly through the tent. Then nothing.

What she had seen had immobilized her. The fiery-haired Elizabeth in the tent with her brother Remy, who lay in the woman's arms like a rag doll as she drank from his neck.

The stunning Vampire looked up, trapping and holding Reggie's gaze, compelling her to enter her brother's tent as she dropped the young man heedlessly to the blanket-covered ground.

When she'd crawled close enough, Elizabeth had taken her hand and pulled her unresisting to her side, rocking her as if she were a child.

"I'm sorry you had to see that." The rich, lilting voice had soothed Reggie's soul with its warmth.

"As I'm sure you are aware, your brother was not a very nice man. And the thoughts he had about you—" Reggie felt the pale arms shudder delicately around her and she nodded in response, knowing that her brother's desires were far from natural. She had, herself, read his thoughts often enough to know that she couldn't ever be alone with him.

"That was the main reason your father was planning to sell you to that ogre of a tradesman. He was concerned you were a witch that would lead his poor boy astray." Her eyes flashed in anger before smiling down at the young Gypsy.

"But we aren't going to let that happen now, are we?" Regina looked up into Elizabeth's jade-colored eyes, her own wide with surprise.

"We aren't?"

Elizabeth shook her head. "No, we are definitely not. You, Regina, will get something you've never gotten before. Something *I've* never gotten. What you've been wanting for a long, long time."

Reggie was bewildered by what she was hearing. How did this woman know so much about her? And what exactly was she offering?

"A choice." After those miraculous words, Elizabeth sunk her fangs deep into Reggie's neck, and suddenly she understood. This amazing being was inviting her to join with them, to become like her, to become a member of her family.

Rapture filled her at the thought of that kind of family, that kind of communion. She would never have to be alone again. Never again be at the mercy of any man. The sensual magick inherent in the feeding thrall wove around the hopeful girl. And she chose.

Elizabeth had turned her into an Unborn that night in the way of their kind. Three times she gave and received blood from the lovely Vampire. Then Reggie lost consciousness.

When she woke she was in another country, in a castle by a beautiful lake at the base of the Italian Alps, surrounded by her new clan. Her three brothers were dead, for they were all criminals with no good in their soul.

Surprisingly, Madame Nicolette had spared Regina's father. She had left him with a clear and complete memory of what had occurred that night. "So that he will live knowing it was his own weakness and ignorance that robbed him of his children." She had serenely answered for her actions. Everyone had nodded in somber agreement. Regina never learned what became of him.

After a day or two, when she realized what she would have to do in order to survive, what she would have to give up, something inside her shattered and cried out in agonized denial. She had made the choice, she knew, but she hadn't truly understood all that it would entail.

"It took me a long time to work up the courage to see Daj Mia. But one night, nearly a year later, I went to her."

It had been a painful experience. Her grandmother had taken one look at her and realized what she had become. Reggie had felt the waves of fear and disgust that instinctively coursed through Mia before she could suppress them.

She heard the unspoken, *"Abomination"*, and she'd known that she had lost the only person whom she'd believed would always love her unconditionally. The pain of that haunted her, even now.

Daj Mia had been dead for one hundred and ninety-two years. Her rejection still hurt as deeply as it had that night. The night Reggie let go of everything she had ever known, let go of the sunlight forever and became a creature of darkness. A Vampire.

Zander picked her up, cradling her against him as he walked towards the waiting shower. She was naked and in his arms beneath the warm spray before she realized where they were going.

He didn't say a word, and for that she was grateful. The trip down memory lane had rung her out emotionally, and she wouldn't have been able to handle discussing anything else right now. Especially not her experience with Grey Wolf. Or the decision she'd come to before arriving at Haven.

Zander began to wash her, inspecting her completely healed back with a grunt of approval before sliding his hands around towards her silken belly. He traced her sun tattoo with a feather-light caress, and she shivered as he journeyed lower, finally easing his soapy fingers between her thighs. Her body's liquid response to his exploration caused her to lean back against him with a sigh.

Her neck arched as he pressed his fingers in a circular motion against her mound before sliding back between the moist lips of her sex. He bent his knees and pressed his rigid erection temptingly between the curves of her bottom, eliciting a shocked gasp at the surprisingly pleasurable sensation. She never imagined—

"Oh yes, you have." She heard his dark, sensual voice clear and amused in her mind. *"And we have lifetimes to make all your fantasies...and mine, come true."*

She trembled as he reached behind him to grab the showerhead, rinsing her off with the pounding liquid. Instantly her muscles began to relax, but she sensed his slightly less than altruistic intentions for the pleasurable hand-held device.

A few moments later, he aimed the massaging jets between her shaking thighs with one hand, the fingers of his other holding her open to the relentless pressure. She cried out at the intensity and felt her knees wobble beneath her. She gripped his forearm to hold her steady as the water pulsed rhythmically against her clit.

Zander's hips rubbed against her instinctively as he shared in the torturous sensations. If he felt this much from her now, he couldn't begin to imagine how much stronger the connection would be once Unity was completed.

Already the bond heightened his arousal and sharpened his

desire to near the breaking point. As she came against him, sending ripples of ecstasy through his body, he knew he had to get inside her.

He replaced the nozzle in its holder, opening the shower door and guiding her out into the steam-filled air of the room. His fingers gripped her chin, turned her head towards him a little roughly to eat at her mouth.

His body covered hers as he leaned her forward until her palms were flat against the cool porcelain of the sink, her legs spread wide. Biting his lip at the sight of her bare and open to his gaze, his fangs broke the skin until he tasted blood. *Mother Goddess, give me strength.*

Her hips lifted invitingly, feet planted firm on the floor. He could sense her impatience. She was as turned on as he was and that knowledge gave him back a modicum of control.

Caressing her hips and back lightly as he watched the moisture gather like dew on silken lips of her sex, feeling her frustration and need mounting with each breathless moment, he waited. He wanted her desperate and aching. He wanted her to need him as he needed her.

"Fuck me, Zander."

His gaze narrowed on her back and his hands tightened on her hips as he heard the taunting whisper. The little seductress was turning the tables on him. Hearing her demand echo through his mind sent white-hot desire pulsing through his veins. His grip tightened as he instinctively pressed closer.

"I need to feel you inside me. Need your cock deep inside my hot, wet—Yes!"

She moaned in triumphant delight when he lifted her hips high, hands clutching her flesh as he plunged his shaft into her with primal force. He held her easily in his grip, her feet dangling in midair, head leaning on her bent forearms as every ounce of his control seemed to disappear. He touched her core with every thrust, felt her inner walls squeeze his cock with a strength that nearly threw him over the edge.

"So good, love, your pussy feels so good."

Mad with lust, he knew he was probably being too rough, using too much of his strength as he filled her. Her words, so intimately given, so hot, had flipped some switch inside him, made him crazed to fuck her hard and fast until she screamed.

He heard her pleasured gasp, felt her body, slick with water and soft beneath his hands, and he knew he wouldn't last long.

Again and again he slammed his hips against her, the wet sound inciting him. He couldn't get enough of the feel of his mate around him. He watched as her heat swallowed him, felt her thighs quiver against his own with each thrust.

She was burning him alive, scalding him with her fire, soaking him with her cream, her muscles tightening around his cock as if begging for more.

Faster.

Deeper.

"More, Zander. More!"

He sensed her inching closer to her climax, and, wrapping one arm around her waist, he used the other to reach around and press her ripe clit between his fingers—applying just the right amount of pressure to push her over the edge.

Her climax hit him with the force of a supernova. They flew together into the sun, burning to cinders before being reborn within the flames.

He placed his open mouth on her shoulder, biting but not breaking the skin, needing to brand her, to mark her. He growled low as he came, his climax joining the power of her own, uniting them in the inferno.

Moments—or hours later, he lowered her boneless legs to the floor, turning her into his arms as they caught their breath in the quickly cooling room.

Emotions he never knew existed flooded through his veins. This determined waif was already more important to him than he could explain or even comprehend. He felt her go rigid in his arms and sighed.

She wasn't ready to hear about what he was feeling. He knew he was really going to need to work on his patience around this little Gypsy.

A wave of irritation came from the handful in his arms before she sent him another message entirely. A strong disturbance had just filled the air, and it was coming from the bar downstairs. From Haven.

He searched through her thoughts and sighed once more, this time in disgust. Pulling back, he leaned his forehead against hers, looking deeply into her worried eyes with a smile.

"You better get down there." Her voice was understandably subdued. There was no way she could have missed the animosity flowing from their new arrivals, animosity directed at her.

The fact that he could sense it so strongly, through her and her unique abilities, was something he would definitely have to think about later. Right now it seemed he had to do his job.

He hugged her quickly before nodding. Grabbing a towel to dry her off, he turned her around, giving her a light smack on the bitable cheeks of her behind with the palm of his hand before wrapping the covering around her damp, tempting body.

At her indignant shriek he laughed, shaking his head with a disappointment that was only slightly feigned. "Okay, I'm going. But later you and I have an appointment for some serious spooning."

71

She gawked at him in disbelief as he continued with an innocent shrug, blues eyes twinkling. "Otherwise I'll just feel used."

Chapter Four

Zander took his time getting dressed. He used the physical act of donning his clothing like an active meditation, calming and centering his mind the way a warrior might before a battle.

He felt his demeanor change. The relaxation and joy he'd experienced in this isolated bubble of time with his mate receded, shoulders straightening as he blanked all expression from his face.

No longer Zander—he was Sariel, Mediator of the Clan Trust and heir to the honorable Sariel Clan.

He caught her watching him as she sat on the bed, already clothed, this time in a flattering ruby skirt and another one of those peasant style blouses that hid her charms from view. "I really do need to go shopping. I think I'd feel tougher, more confident, if I were in my jeans. Or leather. Liz always said you can't help but be kick-ass in leather."

Zander looked up at that and a shadow of a smile graced his lips as he finished buttoning his shirt. He wore the black pants and white long sleeve shirt of a server, his standard uniform.

His reasoning, whenever Lux or his mother would complain about his lack of fashion sense, was that he did in fact work in a pub, and as the Vampire equivalent of Switzerland, he had to be neutral. He didn't want to inadvertently wear the colors of

73

one of the families, showing subconscious favoritism or causing any misunderstandings.

He heard Regina sigh lustily in her head at the sight of him and he realized he'd been waiting for her opinion, was gratified to know she didn't find any fault with what he was wearing. He slumped his shoulders in chagrin. He *really* needed to apologize to his father.

Reggie was feeling as if she'd been struck by lightning. Dazed and a little shocked at her actions, her confessions, not to mention this sudden intimate connection they shared.

She knew so much about him now. How amazing he was. How important to his community. The Mediator, a diplomat like his father before him.

Often it was only Zander Sariel and his ability to moderate between the hotheaded Trueblood families, Were packs and even the occasional Unborn misfit that prevented an all-out war. Something that would not only cause an untold number of deaths amongst their own kind, but the innocent humans that stood unknowingly in their way as well.

She also knew how popular he was with all the female Vampires, not to mention the human women who hung around the pub on the off-chance they would catch his eye. But her jealousy at that information was eclipsed by the inescapable truth that along with her knowing all about him, he now knew all there was to know about her. Even those things she would have rather kept to herself.

When he was ready, she hopped off her perch on the high, soft bed and walked towards the door ahead of him. His surprise and disbelief washed over their connection a moment before he blocked her route, his eyebrow raised in consternation.

"Where do you think you're going?" His tone had her chin tilted up in challenge, hands firmly on her hips. He noted her defensive stance and closed his eyes, pinching the bridge of his nose before he caught her gaze once more.

"Me? I'm going downstairs. That is still allowed, isn't it? Haven is a sanctuary after all. I'm not in any danger inside these walls. Unless," her golden eyes narrowed, "you've decided not to honor your word?"

His insult reached her before he spoke aloud. "A Sariel has *never* rescinded an offer of sanctuary, never purposely put a potential victim in harm's way. So you can pull in your claws, little cat."

Her eyebrow rose at the barb, but she remained silent.

He ran a hand through his neatly combed hair, and she followed the movement. The phrase "sin on a stick" ran through her mind and her heart began to pound as she gazed at the shifting muscles in his arm. Memories of what they'd just done and visions of all she still wanted to do filled her thoughts. He was so strong, so big, and the way he filled her...

"Regina, honey, stop or we'll never get out of here." His voice had deepened with arousal. He took a step closer, as if to pull her into his arms, when she blinked, what he'd said beginning to sink in.

"We?"

He rolled his eyes. "Yes, *we*. But before we walk out that door, we're going to need a few ground rules." She started to argue but he stopped her with a finger to her lips.

"As Mediator, I must be neutral, impartial, if I am to have any authority with the families." The blunt tip of his finger gently caressed her full lower lip as he looked into her eyes, his expression willing her to understand.

"You and I both know that I'm anything but impartial when

75

it comes to you. But if we're to keep you safe, to see which way the winds are blowing in regards to the families and their willingness to fight an enemy they thought already vanquished, let alone a spy in their midst…" He left the sentence hanging, and she realized with a sudden clarity what he was trying to say.

"You have to lie."

His hand left her mouth to clench into a fist at his side upon hearing her words.

"No, Regina. *We* have to be circumspect, hold the cards we have close. If they knew that you were mine, well, that would be the end. The end of my influence, the end of your safety and the end of any chance you have of saving the rest of the Deva Clan. And the traitor helping that Shadow Wolf carry out his plans would never be found. You are Unborn, Regina, and as much as it *doesn't* matter to me, it matters to them."

Regina nodded as if in understanding, but pain pierced her heart at his words. She tried to reason with herself. The only thing that mattered, the whole reason she'd come here in the first place, was to ensure the protection of her clan.

In the heat of the moment, when passions ran high, lust was often mistaken for something deeper, richer than it was. In the end it would be better to keep her emotions separate from her mission.

There was no reason to feel hurt that he wouldn't claim her publicly. He was doing all that she'd hoped he would and more. He'd given sanctuary, he'd saved her life. And as a bonus, he'd given her a few amazing memories. It was foolish to want more.

She moved, turning back towards the door when he pounced. He lifted her high in the air until her back was against the door and placed his mouth on hers.

It wasn't a gentle kiss. It was a kiss of ownership. A kiss of possession and frustration. A kiss that, after a moment of surprised stillness, she participated in greedily, with just as much frustration and fury.

"You are mine, Regina. Make no mistake."

He released her mouth and lowered her slowly to the ground, his chest rising rapidly and his blue eyes flashing with anger and need.

She stood on wobbly legs, desperately trying to catch her breath and recall exactly why she was upset with him. After a moment, resolve straightened her spine and she reached behind her to open the apartment door.

"This should be no problem at all, Zander." She shrugged as she stepped into the hallway. "But you're wrong about one thing. Like I told you before, I don't *belong* to any man. *You* make no mistake about *that*."

Zander stomped down the stairs after her, grumbling. He sounded like a thwarted child as she attempted to leave him behind. This time she was a little too fast, even for him, and she stepped out into Haven one heartbeat before he got to the door.

She almost ran headfirst into Lux. Apparently Zander's brother had been heading up to warn them of the new arrivals. He looked surprised to see them and turned to his brother with a questioning glance. Zander looked pointedly at her, and Lux smiled with understanding and a touch of awe, before taking her hand in his own and bringing it to his lips.

"You just get more fascinating by the hour, Reggie my dear." He lowered his voice before pressing a light kiss to her skin. "Are you sure you wouldn't rather spend the evening with me?"

She smiled as he played the charming rogue, understanding from his clever turn of phrase that she was to stay beside him while Zander dealt with the newcomers. Without turning to glance at the irritated man behind her, she followed Lux to stand beside the bar.

Haven's bartender, who introduced himself in a kind, quiet voice as Joel, was already at her side with an amber glass of liquid courage and a wink.

Lux had obviously told him all about her, and she felt his willingness to befriend her, his admiration, and she could only be grateful. Lux smiled at the young man and she was sure she caught him blush before he turned away to straighten the already perfect row of shot glasses behind the bar. She raised a brow at her escort, but gratefully took a sip before turning to look at the small crowd filling the booth across from her.

Zander went to greet the swanky gathering. Four men and one woman observed him through narrowed eyes. With a look from their leader, three of the men stood abruptly and left the table, sending Reggie looks of thinly veiled contempt as they passed.

Zander sat down beside the remaining couple, a woman and a rather flamboyant man who, in Reggie's opinion, was taking the whole Vampire thing just a little too seriously.

He sported a mass of white blonde hair to his waist, just the right length to fling dramatically over his shoulder, which he did while gesturing to Zander.

The black silk cape flung over the back of the booth was a perfect capper to the loud satin shirt, halfway unbuttoned, of course, and matador-style pants that looked two sizes too small. As he stirred his drink with one delicate hand, pinky elegantly lifted, Reggie snorted into her glass.

She'd be willing to bet money that this particular Trueblood read *way* too many cheesy Vampire novels. She'd never seen a bigger stereotype in her entire life.

She heard a slight choking sound, and looked over just in time to see the woman in the booth patting Zander's back as he choked on the glass of water Joel had deposited at his table. He tilted his head towards Reggie, a warning in his eyes. She must have been projecting her thoughts towards him again unknowingly.

She might have sent him an apologetic thought and blocked her private musings, but her eyes caught and held on the hand that continued to rub suggestively against Zander's back. The female attached to said hand had scooted closer to the handsome Mediator, eating him up with eyes heavily lined with kohl.

She was beautiful, Reggie had to admit. Obviously related to "Vlad the martini drinker", with similar features and the same startling white-blonde hair scraped in a striking upsweep that enhanced her dark doe eyes. Tall and slender—her dress strapless, black and classic—she looked like a runway model.

And if she didn't remove her hand from Zander in the next thirty seconds, she was going to lose it, along with a few hanks of that oh-so-perfect hair.

Reggie watched as Zander stood a little too quickly, moving away from the offending hand under the guise of refurbishing "Vlad's" now empty glass. He walked towards the bar stiffly, the look in his eyes causing her to take a small step towards Lux for safety.

"Don't look to my brother to save you. You are in so much trouble, Regina mine."

Reggie looked up at him innocently as he handed Joel the empty glass. *"I don't know what you're talking about."*

Zander looked at her in disbelief. She heard his silent question as if he were speaking aloud. How was he supposed to hold a serious conversation with the Abbadon family, the heirs of the second most powerful clan in the Trueblood community, with Regina sending such ridiculous, albeit accurate, observations about their young dandy of a son?

"Ah, so you agree with me."

"Whether or not I agree is irrelevant. These are powerful Vampires. They hold sway with the opinions of countless other families."

What she knew he wasn't saying was that they were also the most vocal in their hatred for all Unborns. And Zander was determined to divert them from the current focus of their pique. Namely, her. She wasn't concerned.

"They don't like me? I feel broken inside."

He closed his eyes for a moment, taking a deep, calming breath. He grabbed the fresh drink and turned, and she could sense his attempt to block her random musings from his mind. He was so focused that he almost didn't see the man who'd appeared in front of him.

"This must be the little Unborn we've been hearing so much about. Please introduce us, Sariel. I'm positively filled with...curiosity."

Abbadon stood before the trio, his expression one of disdain. Lux had taken a step forward at the blond's snide tone and she watched as Zander shook his head subtly at his brother.

"Sebastian Abbadon, heir to the Abbadon Clan and all its holdings, respected member of The Clan Trust."

Zander bowed his head slightly in respect before gesturing to her. "May I introduce you to Regina of the Deva Clan, under the protection of the Haven rules of sanctuary...and the personal charge and honored guest of Clan Sariel."

She didn't need to hear the echoing gasps that filled the

pub as she felt the surprise and disbelief that filled the minds of everyone within earshot of Zander's declaration. Even she was aware of what he had done.

By connecting his family name with her safety and protection, he had drawn a proverbial line in the sand. If she was harmed in any way, the Sariel family, and his entire extended clan, would be forced to react as they would to a personal attack. If she was assaulted, the Sariels would enact justice.

To announce something like that so publicly, to offer so great an honor to an Unborn, just *wasn't* done. And Zander knew it, she realized in awe.

He was hoping that it would cause enough of a stir, put enough questions and doubts in the minds of those present, that she would be safe until they could solve this current crisis and he could announce her new status as his *grathita*.

It was the closest he could safely come to claiming her, and she was aware of the risk he was taking. Her anger softened a bit with the knowledge.

Lux smiled his agreement beside her. He threw a challenging look towards Sebastian, whose expression had soured as if he'd swallowed something distasteful.

He quickly overcame his shock, at least outwardly, his features once more smoothing into an expression of charm and pomposity. He bowed formally before Reggie, reaching for her hand as Lux had done only moments before.

Darkness.

Hatred.

Blood and death.

She was inundated with visions and emotions that were so terrible and strong she stumbled a bit from force. His cool, damp lips pressed against her fingertips and she saw it. The face that was as familiar to her as her worst nightmare. Grey Wolf.

Zander took an instinctive step forward, his own surprise at what he'd taken from her mind difficult to conceal. She felt his disbelief, not in what she was sending to him, but in the fact that one of the strongest proponents of Trueblood isolation and most vocal protestor against Werewolf and Vampire alliances could be connected to a Shadow Wolf in the first place.

She saw an image she'd only seen a few times before, in her sire Elizabeth's mind when she thought of her husband Malcolm. Malcolm?

Liz's husband was the previous heir to Abbadon? This prig's late brother?

Zander was remembering him as a dear friend and a celebrated Abbadon warrior. The one who'd been the most successful at destroying the threat *Les Loups De L'Ombre* had offered to the entire Trueblood community no more than six or seven hundred years before.

She was amazed as she felt the objectivity he'd been weaned on at his father's knee take over, allowing him to maintain an appearance of outward serenity. She drew from his deep well of strength, keeping her face expressionless as she gently disengaged her hand from Sebastian's grasp. They both agreed that they couldn't let Sebastian know how her abilities had given him away.

It was obvious now that Grey Wolf hadn't been lying when he'd claimed an alliance with a Trueblood traitor. He was here within arms-reach, the key to finding and destroying her true nemesis. And she could do nothing but pretend ignorance. But she knew that regardless of Haven's rules, to openly attack him without physical evidence would be suicide.

Sebastian's icy green eyes studied her with disturbing intensity. Despite his apparent disgust and lack of respect for her kind, he seemed to find her attractive, if his lascivious thoughts were anything to go by. But along with that attraction, there was a hatred so profound she knew it was only his pretense at civility and fear of reprisal that kept him from drinking her dry. It was a disconcerting realization.

Zander's animosity grew as the other man leered disrespectfully. She tried to reassure him through their link.

His tone was tight with ire as he addressed Sebastian. "Actually, Abaddon, I'm glad you stopped by. Now that we have that little verification of Haven rules out of the way, I'd like to speak to you in my official capacity as Mediator."

She knew then that Sebastian had heard of her arrival and come to question the right of an Unborn to claim sanctuary with the Truebloods. But though they had long since been denied acknowledgement or right to mate with natural Vampires, Unborns were still technically allowed to request aid and protection.

It was within the proprietor of Haven's powers, and his alone, to accept or deny that responsibility. The fact that Zander's family had controlled both ownership of the pub *and* one of the highest generational positions in the Trueblood community gave more weight to his decision.

"I am officially calling for a meeting of The Trust." Zander spoke quietly, his jaw clenched, but his words still sent a shockwave through the small group that surrounded him.

The twelve family heads that made up the Clan Trust met only once every decade. They addressed and evaluated all concerns and requests brought to their attention, and judged any infringements upon clan law. It had been a mere four years since their last gathering, so Zander's pronouncement could only bode ill.

"By what right do you call us?" Sebastian had grown eerily still, his thoughts a confusing jumble of rage and fear that she could barely decipher. He was definitely worried about something.

"By right of *Tarjana*. The families will all be affected by the information Regina has gathered pertaining to...an old enemy."

The curiosity that filled Haven was so palpable she could have sensed it without any special abilities.

Tarjana meant the reason for the impromptu meeting was a threat, a matter of life and death for the clans. She had no doubt all of the clan heads would be informed of the development before the sun had a chance to rise.

Sebastian's internal agitation had increased dramatically, his nod sharp before walking back towards his booth. He took his sister's arm and gestured to the men who had been hovering out of sight.

"It is five days until the next full moon, the soonest a meeting could take place. I will inform the Trust." He looked at Reggie, the fire in his eyes unmistakable. "Let us hope the Unborn isn't misleading us in anyway. The consequences for such a ruse would be dire indeed."

Lux and Zander both tensed beside her, but she could only smile. After facing off with a creature of Grey's caliber—this conceited, hypocritical powder-puff was nothing.

The Abaddon entourage made their exits with just the right amount of drama, and she noticed several other Truebloods following close behind. No doubt they had been listening in, and were heading out to inform their families of the exciting news.

"That was fun." She looked up at the two handsome men beside her. "What now?"

Lux chuckled. "Now, little Reggie, we wait. In five days Zander will tell the family heads what you've learned, and we'll see what those crusty, old stuffed shirts decide to do."

A strong surge of relief washed over her. She knew the fact that the threat from Grey and his pack was directed at all Vampirekind, not just her small family of pariahs, would ensure immediate action on the part of the Truebloods.

And if they showed any hesitation, Zander would make sure they did the right thing. That was just the kind of man he was. She'd done it. What she'd been so determined to do. She'd even been able to discover who the traitor was. Her part in this was done.

"Not so fast, Regina mine." She looked up at the grim tone of Zander's voice. "You are nowhere near done here, so don't even think about leaving. You have to report what you learned directly to The Clan Trust. *You* have to tell them about Grey's plans."

Lux, who'd been standing unknowing beside them, looked startled. "Can she do that? I seem to recall a very strict ruling from the old *Mis*-Trust pertaining to the banning of all non-Truebloods from any official proceedings."

Her eyes narrowed as Zander glared at his brother. "I wouldn't be *allowed* in their presence? So Elizabeth was right about your kind after all. What is the deal with that anyway? I mean, wasn't it a Trueblood or two on the prowl who created the first Unborns? I'll never understand how any of you can actually think you've evolved *beyond* humans. Not when you're just as narrow-minded and arrogant as they could ever hope to be."

She huffed over to the bar where Joel was waiting with a conciliatory shoulder, mumbling under her breath all the while about bloodsucking Nazis.

Lux put an arm around his brother and lowered his voice. "Looks like you have your hands full in more ways than one."

Zander nodded with a sigh as Lux continued. "They're going to eat her alive. Not only an Unborn, not only their Mediator's mate, but a Reader as well. You know what the laws state. A Reader is avoided, hunted to extinction if possible. An Unborn Reader is an abomination that must be disposed of. I don't agree, brother. You *know* that."

He snarled and Lux held his hand up as if to ward off the sound. "But they are nothing if not predictably terrified of change. To discover that Shadow Wolves still roam the land, along with the news of a traitor in our midst, will throw their safe little worlds into a tailspin as it is."

"It's Sebastian." Zander interrupted. "I saw the truth through Regina's link. He knows the Shadow Wolf who tortured her." He saw a rage to match his own light in his brother's eyes.

There was no love lost between the Sariel brothers and the Abbadon heir. He had always been a vicious child, he and his twin causing no end of mischief while their uncles and cousins were away fighting in the war.

Since his brother Malcolm was murdered and he was given the keys to his father's kingdom, Sebastian's sick addictions and narcissistic tendencies boded ill for the future of his clan. That made him everybody's problem. And he'd made it clear how he felt about Zander's family holding such a powerful position.

Up until now, he'd merely been an annoyance. But the possibility that he had anything to do with the being that injured his mate had sealed his fate. There would be a reckoning. It was just a matter of time.

"The Trust will try to discredit her on the basis of her status. They'll try to threaten her and if they find out what she is...they may even try to sentence her to death. But my money's on her. And they are going to have to make a choice. Accept her or lose me as their Mediator. The clan heads aren't foolish. They know our race has been in trouble for centuries. This new threat Regina's brought to light only makes it that much clearer that something needs to change."

Zander shrugged. "Or they can choose to ignore the facts and remain in ignorance. In which case, I hope you're ready to take on the family mantle, little brother."

Lux's face took on a hunted expression. "No way, Zander. This is your destiny, not mine. You'll find a way to make them see reason." Seeming to shake off his concern, Lux rubbed his hands together in anticipation.

"This is one Trust meeting I wouldn't miss for the world. High time for a change too, I'd say. I can't wait. She is certainly bringing some excitement into our lives, isn't she?"

He looked over to make sure that Regina was still distracted by Joel's antics. "When are you going to tell her that leaving is no longer an option?"

"Once Unity is complete and we're officially bonded, I won't have to." Lux tsked teasingly, but didn't disagree. Both knew that nothing could stand in the way of this bonding, not even the stubborn little bride-to-be.

Chapter Five

It had been three days.

Three agonizingly long and frustrating days. Reggie honestly wasn't sure how much more she could stand.

Sure she'd been upset and more than a little tipsy the other night. She raved to Joel and anyone who would listen for hours about the ridiculous, unfair politics and posturing of the Truebloods and how their arrogance was a bit too much for her to stomach.

Thankfully Lux and Joel had protected her as she'd spouted off in drunken frustration. She had felt how many of the regulars wanted to shut her up for good. Maybe she'd gone too far for Zander as well. Ever since then it seemed he had been avoiding being alone with her. And they certainly hadn't had sex since that last unforgettable episode in—and out—of the shower.

She'd woken in his room the past two evenings to find that he'd never even been there. No blanket tossed carelessly across the couch, no lingering warmth beside her on the bed.

He'd said he didn't want to bother her. Claimed she needed her rest in order to fully recover, that he had a lot of preparing to do for the coming Trust meeting.

He'd slept on his brother's couch in the loft apartment across the hall. A development Lux hadn't seemed too happy about. She could only agree. And she wasn't buying his weak excuses. The scariest part of it all was—she couldn't tell.

The side effects of their telepathic hanky-panky seemed to have given Zander some of her blocking abilities. She could sense that he still wanted her. Whenever she saw him she felt the fiery jolt of his desire rip through her system.

She'd been so sure a dozen times in the last few days that he was one breath away from sweeping her upstairs, but something always held him back. And Reggie couldn't for the life of her determine what it was.

Maybe she didn't really want to know. She was terribly afraid that now that he'd had her, he simply didn't want her anymore. Not enough to risk his reputation, his family name. Regardless of all his previous territorial behavior.

Whatever the reason, she was determined to test his self-control tonight. Her stay at Haven was not going to be spent pacing in his rooms wishing for his touch, drinking up all of Lux's blood reserves and eating everything she could get her hands on out of boredom. Tonight she would seduce him.

Nicolette had taught her a few things about the art of tempting a man. She had once been a Madame of great renown. A courtesan of royalty, seducer of kings.

Granted, Reggie didn't have the statuesque blonde's sophistication or elegance, but she could only hope her stubborn determination made up for the lack.

"Men are simple creatures, darling," Nicolette had told her once. "You will find that they are highly competitive in nature, and subtlety is lost on them. If you want a man, and you want to ensure he wants you, you must show him that others want you as well."

Seemed simple enough to Reggie. And with the outfit Joel had snuck up to her rooms, she no doubt looked as though she were wearing a giant "available" sign on her mostly bare chest.

The mirror that framed the inner closet door reflected her dubious expression as she took stock of her "assets".

Long dark hair and almond-shaped eyes lightly framed with a touch of mascara, which only served to enhance the golden hue she'd always despised.

Her lips were too full, in her opinion. And the clinging material of the black dress hugged her curves, plunging shockingly in the front with a hem that ended at her bare upper thighs and made her incredibly self-conscious.

Nicolette could carry this off. Liz wouldn't be caught dead in a dress—she preferred her leather "butt kickers". Reggie? She honestly didn't think she had ever worn anything that showed this much skin. She felt like a little girl playing dress-up. But it would have to do.

Zander had "suggested" she spend the next several days upstairs, away from snooping eyes, away from danger. But tonight, she was going to show him and all those other elitist vamps that Devas don't cower...they dance.

Zander tried to smile politely as he pushed yet another pair of drunk, groping hands from around his waist.

What was it with the female customers tonight? Maybe they'd always been this aggressive and he was just now noticing. He had certainly never minded the attention before. But everything seemed different now. He knew that he'd probably be repeating that phrase a lot from now on. Everything *had* been different...before Regina.

He wondered for the umpteenth time if she was as pained by their forced separation as he was. Did she miss him? Did she even care? He honestly wasn't sure.

He knew he'd hurt her with what she'd seen as his initial rejection, but since then they'd barely spoken. The only glimpses of his *grathita* came when she'd popped down to grab a tray of food, or talk to Joel or his brother.

But he sensed her, smelled her, could practically taste her on his tongue. He relived their time together over and over in his mind, until he was sure he'd go insane with wanting her. But he had to be strong.

He'd told Lux he would complete the Unity and let her handle the repercussions after the fact, but it hadn't taken him long to realize if he did that, he'd be no different than every other person that had come before him. He would be taking away Regina's right to choose.

As far as he was concerned—as far as genetics was concerned—there really was no choice. There would be no other *grathita* for him. The powers that be only supplied one Trueblood mate. But she still had a choice.

Until the third and final joining of body and blood, where they would truly be one, she still had a chance to say no.

After that, there would be no hidden mental corners between them. Their lifespan would be shared and they would have a biological need to be near the other, to partake in each other's life force.

It would hurt them both, physically and mentally, to deny that communion. But there were recorded instances where it had been done. And while everything in him screamed out in denial at his decision, he knew there was a part of her that would never forgive him for taking that choice away, and he couldn't start their life together with that between them. He wouldn't.

"Hey, roomie, having fun with your groupies?" Zander turned to glare at Lux in ill humor, the answer clear in his eyes.

Lux smiled, his handsome face the picture of innocence, which instantly made Zander suspicious.

"You wouldn't happen to know why I've been propositioned more since sundown than I have in the last decade would you, brother?"

Lux looked down at his fingernails and up at the ceiling, before peeking sideways at his imposing brother. "I may have told one or two of the regulars that you were a little lonely and depressed over a breakup and could use some female companionship."

Zander growled and Lux's expression changed to one of frustration. "Is it a lie? Is it just my imagination that you haven't spoken to your *grathita* in days, haven't finished the bonding process? Have I been having delusions of you moping around the pub, around *my* rooms as if the end of the world was looming?"

Lux lowered his voice. "I understand your reasons, Zander, I really do. I even respect them, misguided though they may be. But you left someone out of the loop, and I don't think she's come to the same conclusions."

Zander looked up, startled. He paled as Lux rolled his eyes. "You have always been the one to see the bigger picture Zander, I can't believe you didn't realize that with you holding all your emotions back from her, she might have no choice but to take your actions to heart."

He looked over his brother's broad shoulder, his eyes widening. "Or that you didn't wonder about how she might retaliate." He grabbed Zander's shoulder before he could turn and see what had drawn Lux's lustful glance.

"I just came over here to tell you that I'm...entertaining tonight. You'll have to find some other place to curl up and sigh in melancholy dejection."

He started to walk away and paused. "Oh, and I called in Nita for the night. Joel's busy." Zander raised one brow in sardonic acknowledgment, understanding what his brother wasn't saying. It bothered him to no end that his brother would be enjoying a passion-filled evening while all he had to look forward to was unsatisfying dreams and empty arms.

A sultry, innuendo-laced number emerged from the deejay's sound system. It had him wondering what Regina was doing at that moment. Was she lying in his bed even now, imagining all the things he'd done to her? Or, more likely, was she cutting up all his clothing and cursing his name for being an arrogant ass?

He was seriously considering taking the final decision of joining out of her hands, to hell with his good intentions. That's when he felt it. The room suddenly filled with electricity, a palpable sense of expectation and excitement. *Shit.*

He turned slowly, as if in a dream. His knees actually went weak, though he'd never admit that to anyone in a thousand years. The only thing stopping him from rushing towards her and carrying her away as fast as his abilities would allow was the suspicion in the spying eyes he could feel even now. Observing his every reaction, looking for weakness.

How on earth was he supposed to protect her when she came into a room filled with hungry predators looking like dessert?

That dress, what there was of it, was lethal. The women who came into Haven often dressed to entice, but none of them held a candle to Regina. She was temptation. The personification of desire. He had to get her out of here.

"Regina, you need to go back up to our rooms right now."

From the other side of the room he could see her chin lift in defiance. *"Long time no hear, Sariel. I was bored in your rooms and thought I'd come down and get a little...action."*

Zander took two steps forward but Joel beat him to the punch, looking at his employer reproachfully as he steered Regina towards the dance floor. Lux quickly followed and Zander watched as a dancing Regina was placed between the two men, the three of them enjoying themselves a bit too much for his peace of mind.

Joel had Zander's mate pressed up against his front, hands on her swaying hips. Lux sidled up behind the grinning goddess, whispering in her ear, making her laugh, which caused several fascinated eyes to turn her way.

Regina leaned her head back on Lux's shoulder as she chuckled, pressing her hips teasingly against Haven's soon to be ex-bartender in the process.

Every cell in Zander's body rejected what he was seeing, demanding he lay public claim to this maddening woman. He knew his brother would never attempt to steal his blood mate, but he wasn't entirely sure Joel or Regina had gotten the memo.

It could be worse. One of the many less than honorable pub-goers whose gazes were currently turned his woman's way could take her up on her unknowing invitation. And then, all this subterfuge would be for naught. He would be forced to pummel whoever touched her into an unrecognizable pile of flesh.

"Well, your little project looks like she's settling in fairly well. And it seems as though brother Lux hasn't wasted any time marking his territory."

He didn't need to turn to know who stood beside him. Sari Abbadon, Sebastian's twin and a never-ending thorn in Zander's side.

They'd been lovers for one ill-conceived moment in time more than a century ago, but she still behaved as if their separation was only temporary, as if he would soon come to his senses and return to her patiently waiting arms.

Sari wanted an alliance of power, and was one of the many in their community who either didn't believe in, or no longer cared about finding her Trueblood mate.

Not for the first time, he thought that something would soon have to change in their stagnant community, or they would politically maneuver themselves into extinction. There had to be a way to get through to The Trust.

"Sari. Where's your brother?" He wasn't really paying attention to her reply, too busy watching as Lux whirled Regina around to face him, looping his fingers through Joel's jeans and pulling him forward, until the three were pressed together tightly as they swayed to the primitive beat of the music.

His blue eyes narrowed dangerously on the young Joel, whose face was flushed with enjoyment and lust. The only thing that saved him was the deejay's wise decision to end the torturous song in favor of something with a harder beat.

Sari's hand on Zander's chin wrenched his gaze away from the trio to face her obvious irritation. "What is so fascinating about that worthless little Gypsy?" She pouted prettily, her expression meant to entice, but falling far short of the mark. "She's been all Sebastian and my father can talk about, you can't take your eyes off her and Lux is obviously getting more from her than her dirty Unborn blood."

Her faced paled and she gasped in pain before he realized he held her thin wrist tightly in his grip. Jerking his chin out of her hold, he dropped her arm in disgust.

Backing her towards the door with his large frame, he spoke in a harsh whisper. "You insult my family and those under my protection with your jealous and spiteful words. Because of my respect for your sire and the debt I still owe to your elder brother, *may his soul rest with the Mother*, I will not

95

embarrass you by throwing you out in the street for all to see as you so richly deserve. Unless of course you don't leave my establishment in the next five minutes."

Sari's jaw dropped as she glanced surreptitiously around to make sure no one had heard his blunt ultimatum. Then her dark eyes narrowed with malice and her thin arms snaked quickly around his neck as she pressed her lips to his.

It took him a few moments to get over his shock before he pried her clinging limbs loose and pushed her away. Whatever she saw in his expression must have warned her of his intent, because she stepped away quickly, grabbing her wrap from a nearby booth before leaving Haven without a single word or backward glance.

He ignored the curious looks of those who passed him, taking a deep breath before turning to face the crowded dance floor once more. He couldn't see Regina anywhere.

His mind reached out to hers...she was in the booth closest to the deejay, alone. His shoulders slumped in relief.

Lux and Joel had both disappeared. Zander had a pretty good idea as to where they'd gone. Exactly where he was planning to go as soon as he conferred with Nita and made arrangements to close up early. No more waiting. It was time for Regina to choose.

He could only pray she chose him.

"Is he watching?"

Reggie tried desperately not to look away from Joel's twinkling hazel eyes as she spoke to the man currently grinding behind her.

"Yes, I do believe he is. And by the look in his eyes I'd say our little plan is working perfectly."

Joel glanced worriedly over Reggie's shoulder at Lux, who merely chuckled and pretended to whisper in her ear as he spoke to his current paramour.

"Don't look so nervous, Joel. Neither your job nor your life is in any current danger. Your virtue, on the other hand..." He tickled Reggie lightly until she laughed with him, leaning her head back against him as they danced.

She'd asked them to help her in her plan to entice Zander back to her bed. It was amusing how quickly and eagerly the two had jumped in to aid her in her mission. Joel had even gone shopping for her. She knew their actions weren't entirely selfless. At least, in Lux's case they weren't.

This distance between her and Zander was putting a definite crimp in the bachelor's style. But still, she was grateful to them both for helping. She wasn't foolish enough to think she could just walk into a room full of strangers, most of them Trueblood Vampires, and remain safe should Zander not come to the correct conclusions in time.

She had to admit, it was no hardship being pressed between these two incredibly sexy specimens of masculinity, having their attention focused solely on her.

Well, not solely. They were just as focused on each other. And to her surprise, that fact was far more arousing than she would have ever suspected. Especially when Lux began to verbally seduce his lover, with her in the middle.

"Isn't she beautiful, Joel?" Lux turned her to face him, pressing her against his hardening groin and pulling Joel closer behind her in the process.

"And she's definitely giving me ideas." His blue eyes seemed to glow with excitement. "I'm thinking you and I should invite one of those recently scorned ladies by the bar to join us upstairs. Imagine all the delicious things we could do to her. All the things we could do to each other."

The decadent images coming from the two men sped through her and stole her breath. Apparently, Joel was more than pleased with that idea. In their minds they had both placed Reggie in the still unknown female's position.

Her pupils dilated as she stared into Lux's eyes. With his dark, fiery hair falling forward to caress his cheeks, his sensual lips, he really was a stunningly beautiful man. If she hadn't met Zander, she had no doubt she would have been yet another willing victim of his magnetism.

"I am happy that my brother has found such a prize in his *grathita*. He has always been the lucky one. But I have to admit," he leaned closer to her until their lips were a single breath away, "a part of me wishes things had turned out differently."

She smiled crookedly in agreement as he backed away. While she'd been up in the apartment alone, Lux had come to visit several times, and she'd finally convinced him to explain all the confusing sentiments and imagery she'd gotten from Zander's mind about *grathitas* and Unity.

It was difficult to believe at first, a bit overwhelming, but she'd known from her own reaction to their current separation that it was the truth. Zander was her mate. Or he would be if they shared blood once more. She still wasn't exactly sure how the whole thing worked. Or if he still wanted her.

Lux was positive he did, that it was ridiculous for her to doubt what she'd felt with her own abilities. But she'd been hurt so many times, rejected by people she'd believed truly loved her. It was hard for her to trust.

All she knew was, regardless of all her previous plans to disappear for the good of her clan, and despite the hardships she knew were coming...she wanted to be with Zander. She wanted to belong to him. To be his *grathita* in truth. Hence the elaborate scheming, which wasn't having the exact effect she'd been counting on, at least not for Zander.

She felt Lux's impatience and Joel's excitement and knew she couldn't force them to continue the farce.

Stepping out from between them as the music changed and focusing for a moment, she pointed towards a small but rather voluptuous woman who was standing by the bar. The lady was looking as if she was used to being invisible as she tugged self-consciously on the plunging neckline of her sweater.

"That woman's name is Molly. She's feeling a little insecure because all of her friends have hooked up with someone for the evening. On an interesting note, one of her fantasies just happens to be exactly what you boys have in mind." She felt a moment's guilt for picking out the woman's personal thoughts, but consoled herself with the knowledge that she would soon be on the receiving end of unimaginable pleasure because of it.

Joel took in the raven-haired Reggie with awe. Lux merely smiled and kissed her cheek. "As I said, Zander has all the luck. Do you want me to walk you over to him before he makes a scene?"

They both turned towards the object of their discussion. She felt something in her heart break.

Zander wouldn't be making any scene. Not with her anyway. He was far too busy kissing the lips off Sari Abbadon.

Lux had told Reggie all about her too. The old flame. The spoiled princess. The Trueblood with whom it was apparently all right to make out with in public. She turned away and headed for an empty booth near the stage.

Lux tried to follow but she stopped him. All her mental blocks were precarious enough as it was, if he stayed to offer sympathy they might crumble altogether, and she didn't want

Zander's pity.

She forced herself to smile. "We'll work it out, Lux, I promise."

She tapped her head with a watery laugh. "I do have the home-field advantage, you know. Besides, you have plans you need to get to, and a woman who is seconds away from leaving and missing the best night of her short, human life."

Lux didn't look entirely convinced, but after a frustrated glance at the hovering Joel, he nodded. Placing a firm kiss on her surprised lips he turned and walked away, the eager bartender close behind.

She closed her eyes and lay her head in her hands. She should have known. Men were so fickle. How many times had Nicolette told her so? And she'd been a fool to think an Unborn could ever win his heart, no matter that some spiritual link was supposed to be pulling them together. No matter how her Gypsy heart had wanted to believe that Daj Mia's stories about soul mates were true.

"Are you well, Miss?" Reggie looked up into the face of a beautiful young man. Human. He didn't look as if he could be any older than she was when she was turned. She stared blankly for a moment, her hesitation the only invitation he seemed to need as he sat down beside her.

She could sense his attraction. He was a willing donor. Groupies, Lux called them. The sexual satisfaction found in the thrall *was* addictive to humans, almost like a drug to many of these regulars. And harmless, as long as the recipients restrained themselves from taking too much.

He was also very brave. The other humans had been warned to stay away from her by their "special friends", that to offer her any sustenance would lead to punishment. But this young man had seen her sitting here, isolated and sad, and had risked his top spot in the pecking order to offer her solace.

"I offer myself freely." The boy's youthful smile was enticing as he swept his long hair, dyed black to match his fingernails and the rest of his Goth garb, over one shoulder, leaning forward to offer his neck.

She stared, hypnotized by the excited pulse of the veins beneath his pale skin. She hadn't had anything beyond synthesized blood in days—and there was a difference. The warmth of a living body, the richness of the life force as it flowed. So much more satisfying than the imitation. It was like comparing a rice cake to rich, dark chocolate.

When she began to lean forward, to catch the scent of his blood—it happened. A scream of denial and disgust rose up from the depths of her soul, her stomach roiled and every fiber of her being rejected the mere idea of accepting blood from anyone other than her blood mate.

Zander. She recalled what Lux had said about the connection. He'd warned her this would happen. She was addicted to Zander. He alone could fulfill her need for blood now. No other living being would do. And he no longer wanted her. How was that for irony?

Reggie touched the young man's shoulder and shook her head, a kind smile on her face to soften the rejection. He looked confused for a moment, but then he smiled and nodded, sliding out of the booth and disappearing into the throng on the dance floor, in search of his fix.

She wasn't sure how long she sat there, left thankfully alone, but she was startled out of her reverie by the bartender's announcement of last call. It seemed early, but she was so lost in thought she didn't think much of it.

Rising quickly, she swept past the grumbling clientele who were shuffling towards the exit, entering the private stairwell with a sigh.

She decided she would sleep on the sofa. It was torture being surrounded by the scent of Zander on the pillow beside her, in the sheets. The memory of their lovemaking kept sleep at bay. She wasn't worried that she might run into him. Since seeing that lip lock, she was fairly certain they had gone somewhere together. And she refused to mentally seek him out. She did have a little pride left.

At the top of the stairwell where Lux and Zander's apartments diverged, she felt it. Desire. Need. Three minds focused on one goal. *Pleasure.*

She found herself walking trancelike towards Lux's rooms. Her curiosity titillated, she didn't stop to consider her inappropriate actions as she silently turned the doorknob.

She peered in from the darkened entryway. Lux's rooms were set up exactly like Zander's, so from this vantage point she had a clear view of the sitting area and the bed.

Standing in the center of the room was the trio, in various states of undress, so involved in what they were doing that she doubted they would notice if a hurricane swept into the room, let alone one tiny voyeur.

Chapter Six

As the threesome stood entwined in their erotic tableau, Reggie felt the breath seize in her lungs. It was a scene of forbidden beauty, intensely sensual, and her body responded in kind.

Lux had pulled back his thick, shoulder-length hair, his beautiful face tight with restraint and need as he watched the already naked Joel slowly undressing their prize.

Molly, Reggie recalled the woman's name. She watched Joel reveal her curving flesh slowly, looking to Lux with every gesture as if for approval.

While Lux reached out to caress the newly bared flesh, Regina studied him. He was bare from the waist up, his body leaner than Zander's, but impressive nonetheless. Both his arms were sleeved from shoulder to wrist in the most fascinating spiral tattoos she had ever seen.

His smooth chest was marred only by the small silver bars piercing his dusky nipples. He looked so primitive, so overtly sexual, that Reggie had a hard time not responding to his magnetic pull.

He stepped behind Molly as Joel removed the last of her clothing, his hands cupping her abundant breasts. She leaned back against him. Joel, on his knees before the couple, looked up expectantly, his hands clenched on his thighs.

One clothed leg pressed between Molly's thighs, spreading them slightly as Lux's hands lowered, gliding over her stomach to tease the light brown curls below. Molly moaned in anticipation, planting her feet further apart, silently begging him to continue.

"Joel wants to taste you. To see if you're as sweet as you look." Lux slid one thick finger between her trembling thighs, smiling when she gasped.

"It seems she likes that idea." He raised the now damp finger to his lips, his eyes closing as he savored her taste. Looking down at the coiled man below him, he nodded.

Joel grinned up at the panting woman, his hands gripping her hips gently as he leaned into his task.

Reggie fell back against the wall, one hand pressed against her pounding heart, the other clenched low on her belly as she saw the sweet, eager Joel drink from the woman's glistening mound. Lux's hands had returned to her breasts, his lips caressing the nape of her neck as they all watched Joel feast.

Reggie allowed her mind to open, allowed the thoughts and emotions racing through Molly's mind to flow through her. Closing her eyes, she could see through Molly's as Joel lapped her clit affectionately, licking at her labia with broad swipes of his agile tongue.

She felt more than saw Lux's sudden nakedness against Molly's spine as she shared the human woman's experience. Her surprise was palpable, and Reggie smiled at the reminder of the talent the Sariel brothers seemed to share for making clothing disappear.

He bent his knees and placed the tip of his rigid shaft against her heat. Regina opened her eyes as she heard the dual moans of Molly and Joel. He pressed forward, filling the woman with his thick cock. Molly cried out at the overwhelming sensation.

Joel pulled her closer, dipping his head further between her legs to include Lux in his wicked ministrations. Lux growled his pleasure at the feel of the tight heat clasped around him, Joel's tongue flicking out to caress his arousal with every thrust.

As the two men continued to bombard Molly with their sensual attack, she came for them. But they weren't satisfied with a single climax. They were tireless.

Time ceased to have meaning as they pushed her past the brink over and over until she sagged, exhausted, against them. Lux gently disengaged his still rock-hard erection, laying her on the bed, her legs dangling weakly off the edge. He kissed her lips tenderly, then turned his attention to Joel.

"He has an amazing mouth, doesn't he, Molly?" He took his cock in hand, still wet from the spent woman's arousal, and began to stroke himself almost casually.

Joel's gaze followed his movements with rapt attention. As did Reggie's. This was her first full view of Lux and she was able to see exactly why Molly had been so caught between pleasure and pain. It must run in the family, she thought, her golden eyes widening further at the sight.

"And he loves to use it too. But I know what he'd like to do even more. He wants to fuck you, sweet, and I'm going to let him. Just as soon as he gives me what I want." Lux stepped closer to Joel, sliding the head of his erection against the panting man's mouth.

Molly, her back elevated by pillows, watched along with Reggie in fascinated wonder as, after another nod from Lux, Joel parted his lips further to allow him entrance.

It was the most wickedly beautiful thing she had ever seen, watching Lux's cock disappearing into Joel's mouth. It was obvious they were both enjoying themselves.

Lux had thrown back his head, his mouth opening on a silent gasp, incisors elongated in his passion, hands clenched tightly in Joel's hair.

The young bartender was more vocal in his pleasure, humming as if Lux was the best thing he had ever tasted, reaching up to pull him closer, taking every inch of the well endowed man as deep as he could go and swallowing around him.

"Mother Goddess, *yes*. That's it. Take it all and imagine how good it's going to feel when you're finally fucking her...and I'm fucking *you*." Joel moaned loudly at the dark words, his flushed cheeks hollowing as he suckled Lux's shaft with a ferocity that was apparently all the other man could take as he jerked away from Joel's mouth.

Grabbing his shoulders, Lux pulled Joel up into a fiery kiss, thrusting his tongue aggressively into his mouth, licking the droplets of blood they had both caused by the careless mashing of lips and sharpened fangs.

Molly, her need revived by the act of watching the two men together, was caressing her breast with one hand, rubbing her mound slowly with the other. Lux turned Joel towards her, placing the painfully erect man between her open thighs. Joel leaned over her, his eyes glued to her hand as it continued to fondle one generous breast.

Reggie saw Lux reach out, picking up a small tube of some kind from where it sat on the table. Bending Joel over even further, he began to speak. "You've earned your prize with that gifted mouth of yours. You may enter her, Joel. But don't move, and no coming until I say." Molly moaned in frustration at this, but Reggie could feel Joel's energy vibrating with barely suppressed anticipation.

This was what he'd been waiting for. This was what he

wanted.

Joel entered Molly smoothly, beaming appreciatively before licking the nipple she'd been neglecting.

He tensed as Lux stepped closer, running his hand down the young man's back, caressing one quivering flank before drenching his fingers with the contents of the tube.

His fingers slid slowly, almost tauntingly between Joel's cheeks, separating them before pressing inward, pushing through the tight ring of muscles, first one finger then two, teasing him, readying him for what was to come.

Reggie had never before witnessed this kind of carnality. Her trembling limbs had long since collapsed beneath her, need escalating to the point of pain. She knew she shouldn't be here, but she couldn't move, couldn't look away.

Her legs squeezed tightly together, feeling the moisture of her arousal dampening her thighs, holding her breath as she watched Lux replace his thrusting fingers with the plum-shaped head of his cock.

The three bodies were frozen for a moment and Regina held her breath as she waited for what would come next.

Joel, his impatience and need exploding within him, made the first move. Pressing powerfully backward, he impaled himself on Lux's waiting shaft. He cried out as Lux roared in surprised pleasure.

Smacking an alabaster cheek before leaning over Joel's back once more, one hand clenched on his hip, the other gripping the groaning man's shoulder, Lux spoke in a voice harsh with need.

"I believe I told you not to move. You should probably be punished." He thrust his hips jerkily, gasping as Joel apparently did something around Lux's flesh that Reggie couldn't see.

"Maybe later," Lux rasped, before driving his shaft deep into the ecstatic man, the motion thrusting them as one against the waiting Molly, whose legs wrapped around them both and held on tight.

Reggie felt her own hand sliding beneath her dress, the need to join them in their mad rush to the finish line paramount. Her hand immediately drenched with her own juices as she massaged her clit, trying to ignore the niggling disappointment that it was her hand, and not Zander's, bringing her to climax.

"All you had to do was ask."

Before she had a chance to gasp he was there, one hand over her mouth, the other swiftly joining her own beneath the skirt of her small black dress.

"Zander?" Reggie felt her face heat as she realized that he must have known where she was, what she'd been doing this whole time.

How could she not have sensed him? How was it that he kept slipping through all her defenses, yet he could hold his mind back from her? And why wasn't he with Sari?

"How could you think I'd gone anywhere with her, Regina mine? If you took one minute to read me as you do everyone else, you'd know the only woman I want is the one I'm holding right now."

His words halted, rough with need as he slid his fingers through her sopping folds. *"You're so wet, my love. So wet and hot and so incredibly aroused. Do you like watching them? Do you want me inside you that way? It would be so good, Regina. I'd make you feel so good."*

A moan bubbled up from her chest but she held it back, afraid to alert the others to their presence. Having Zander with her, watching her reactions, heightened the excitement of the moment, that sense of the forbidden. She'd never been so aroused.

"I need to touch you, all of you, Regina mine. Don't make a sound. Watch them, my love. Watch and let me bring you pleasure."

She may have nodded, swallowing as she opened her eyes to watch as Lux shafted the duo on the bed, his muscles rippling with the power of his aggressive, sure movements.

Zander shifted her up onto her knees, legs spread as he raised her dress to her hips. *"I love you like this, all open and wet and ready for me. If I'd known you weren't wearing anything underneath this dress in the pub, I may have killed Joel for touching you."*

He slid two fingers inside her, grazing her clit with his thumb, teasing her with slow strokes until she instinctively pressed against his hand, desperate for the release he could give her.

"Impatient, Regina? Isn't this what you wanted? What you wished for as you touched yourself? Or did you want something...more?"

Continuing the slow, torturous movements of his fingers inside her, he used his other hand to press between her shoulder blades. Her torso sunk until she was on her elbows, her lower body bare and open to his gaze.

His satisfied purr rumbled through her mind. He dipped low and nipped at her thighs, licking the dew of her arousal from the pale flesh before seeking its source. Quick, fluttery flicks of his tongue teased her clit, disappearing before she could find satisfaction.

She sent him a threatening visual but he just chuckled darkly through their connection, raising his head to replace his mouth with his thick fingers, thrusting two deep inside her, causing her to arch, catlike, against him.

He gathered her moisture with his other hand, pressing one digit firmly against her anus, pushing inside, just as she'd seen Lux do to Joel.

Her eyes widened, the sensory overload of watching the sexual orgy before her, sensing their excitement and feeling Zander's invading fingers almost too much to take.

Yes.

"That's what you wanted isn't it, Regina mine? Me inside you...filling you here. You're so tight around my fingers. I can't wait to feel you wrapped around my cock. It's been too damn long."

Her hands curled on the cool wood floor as he filled her front and back. He continued his relentless assault, the slight pinch and tingling fullness as he added a second finger to the first inside her, so totally alien and yet at the same time so thrilling.

She tried to breathe, to relax her muscles as he stretched her, readied her for more. Licking and nibbling lightly on her neck as both hands thrust in time with the trio on the bed, he brought her over the edge.

Sparks of fire raced up her spine and she bit her lip to hold back her cry of completion. Her fangs broke through the fragile skin, filling her gasping mouth with the taste of her own blood.

She noticed Lux raise his head from his task, nostrils flaring as he continued to pound against Joel and the climaxing Molly.

His head turned, blue eyes flaring with a surprise that quickly turned to excitement as he saw the duo crouched in the darkness, Regina naked from the waist down.

"Now!" Lux groaned as he bent his knees to deliver one final powering thrust. The permission was all Joel needed, his climax stiffening his frame as Lux joined him, biting into his neck as he spent himself inside his lover.

Joel as well had sunk his fangs into the swell of Molly's breast, causing her to climax once more along with them. It was a sight Regina would not soon forget.

An instant later Regina found herself back in Zander's rooms, safely draped across his legs on the sofa as she trembled with the aftershocks of her passion. They were both silent for long moments, calming their racing heartbeats, lost in thought.

Her face flamed. Lux had seen them! He'd scented her blood, sensed her as she came. Knew she'd been a witness to their intimate ménage.

"It's all right, Regina. My brother is quite the exhibitionist. I'm fairly certain he enjoyed knowing you were there." She tried to get up from Zander's lap but soon realized she wasn't going anywhere until he decided otherwise, and he seemed perfectly content with the current arrangement.

"Might as well stop struggling, love. We need to talk and you have a very nasty habit of running away from me. We're not moving from this spot until we get a few things straight."

Though she raised her eyebrow at his autocratic tone, she nodded, curiosity keeping her silent.

Leaning back against the couch with his warm armful, Zander attempted to push his arousal aside. He shifted uncomfortably as his erection pressed against her barely clothed behind. He needed all his wits about him. The next few minutes could very well be the most important of his life.

It wasn't in his nature, or any Vampire's for that matter, to *ask* for a commitment. It was something Truebloods took for granted. A *grathita* just was, there were no formal proposals. He felt his stomach knot with unaccustomed nerves. Where to begin? And how?

"I'd like it if you start with why you were kissing your ex-girlfriend—the albino. Or why you haven't come near me for days."

He rolled his eyes, pulling her closer so he could lean her head on his shoulder. "If you're finally paying attention to my thoughts again, you'll know how ludicrous your jealousy is. Sari kissed *me*. I have no clue as to why, since I was in the middle of kicking her out of Haven. I have absolutely no interest in her, or anyone else for that matter. As to the reason I've given you some breathing room...that's what I want to talk to you about."

Reggie snuggled closer unconsciously, his scent surrounding her, reminding her how very much she'd missed it, missed him. She had to admit, she was having an easier time sensing his thoughts. Maybe she'd been the one putting up obstacles all along. She'd been too unsure of herself, too afraid to find out what he was really thinking.

"But you know what I'm thinking now, don't you?"

She blushed at the graphic visual he sent her, her body warming once more as she lifted her face to his for a kiss.

His reaction shocked her. Leaning away from her reaching mouth, he placed his hand on her head, pressing her down into the crook of his neck once more.

Her instinctual hurt was washed away as she felt his tension. Whatever Zander wanted to discuss was obviously important to him. She slid her hand up to one broad shoulder, squeezing affectionately before sliding down his arm to take his hand in her own.

"When I was young, my mother used to tell me of the Moon Mother and the creation of the first Vampires, have you ever heard the story?" She remained silent, instinctively knowing he had not expected an answer.

Within moments she was lost in his magical tale. It was the story Nicolette always referred to but never shared, a story that tickled the edges of her long-ago memories. Memories of Daj Mia and the fireside tales she had spun for a golden-eyed child.

"When the earth was new, and humans still fighting with sticks and the intricacies of fire, the Mother looked down from her home in the stars and was concerned. She worried for the frail beings that she and the other gods had created. So susceptible to the wild things that roamed the land, such short life spans filled with so much illness and hardship.

She decided to create guardians, beings that could tame the beasts of the wood and monsters of the air. A species of man that was stronger, more evolved, who would be able to protect his fragile brethren from harm.

One species endowed with the spirit and abilities of the wolf, the ruler of the forest and the Mother's favored animal companion.

Strength and stamina, longevity and loyalty were but a few of his gifts. He would be the Werewolf, able to walk as man *and* animal, to live in both worlds. A bridge between man and beast, protector of all.

The other species was Vampire. They too could shift and communicate with animals and humans alike, though their spirits were not as tied to the natural world.

They too had superior strength and were exceedingly long-lived. They could control the skies, the weather and often, the minds of any who would do harm to those under their protection.

The two were meant to work together. To keep themselves hidden and separate from their charges, allowing humanity to thrive without undue interference. To live on the periphery as they guarded the fragile beings the gods so loved.

For a time it seemed the Mother's experiment was a success.

Like angels on the earth, her guardians kept human beings safe from harm. Healing them and teaching them under the guise of wise men and shamans, giving them the knowledge of nature's plants and healing herbs, leaving them none the wiser.

They kept the predators away and the humans grew, filling the land with their number, dying only from old age, as the Mother had decreed.

Civilization blossomed. Great structures rose from stone and sand, and man became ruler of all he surveyed, taming the wild forests and conquering elements.

More humans meant more housing, more tilling of the ground and destruction of the wilderness. More worshippers meant more temples, more offerings to the gods that had created them.

The Werewolves, those men and women who felt the plight of the natural world, attempted to slow the expansion. They argued that there was room for all—that the Mother had gifted them with abundance enough to share.

When their words went unheeded by man and Vampire, who applauded and promoted the spreading of intellectual pursuits and civilization, the forest dwellers took action.

The villagers watched in disbelief as the monstrous visions attacked their homesteads, killing their livestock and, after they'd developed a taste for blood, killing their neighbors as well. They prayed and sacrificed and looked on in horror. What had they done to so anger the Mother?

Vampires were sent to restore balance. Their secret distaste for their fellow guardians tainted their hearts, and they enacted justice with a telling zealousness, using the powers the Mother had given them to kill.

First, only those that had been guilty of violence against the humans...but guilt soon became irrelevant. Soon both sides forgot the reason for the battle, and winning became their one all-consuming obsession.

When the humans saw the powerful beast-men, when they saw the men who controlled the skies and enthralled their brothers and sisters, compelling them to do their bidding without thought, they were terrified and humbled.

They turned their eyes from the sky and began to worship the gods who walked the Earth. The Mother, who had once been so quick to come to the aid of man, watched in silence.

The Wolf 'gods' and the Vampire 'gods' continued warring with each other, killing humans senselessly in their pride-filled battles meant to determine who was the more powerful, who deserved to rule.

Still the Mother watched in silence.

But she came to a favored few in dreams. She filled the minds of those human beings who had remained loyal to her. Women who had tirelessly prayed in the temple for salvation from the false gods. To them she gave special knowledge and abilities.

She taught them how to use the power she'd hidden in the minds of man. She taught them how to kill her once-beloved creations. And she waited.

The oppressed humans rose up against their false gods, lead by the loyal followers of the Mother. The deity did nothing to protect her guardians from the massacre that followed.

Many Weres and Vampires died. The few remaining hid in

caves or far beneath the ground, embittered and weakened. Only then did the Mother return to her children one last time.

For their arrogance and disobedience, She enacted her punishment. Since they could not be trusted away from her watchful eye, they would both be tied irrevocably to the symbol of her reign. The moon.

The spirit of the wolf that dwelt within each *Were* would hold more sway under its light, for the wolf was by far the more loyal and honorable, and perhaps the *Weres* would learn how to live together in harmony at last.

The Vampire, with all his vast powers and abilities, would be trapped beneath her light for all time. Sunlight would bring weakness and pain, their only strength would be found in the darkness.

And the humans to whom they'd been so cruel, they would now protect more vehemently, for they would be forced to live in symbiosis with them if they were to survive. To share in their life force, with the knowledge that to take too much blood from any human would mean death for them both.

The Mother had one more surprise for the guardians. To ensure that neither species would ever again be equal in number to human beings, they would no longer be able to procreate... not unless they were paired with their one true mate.

She assured them that somewhere in the world, during their lifetime, would be the one soul that would make them whole. And it was only within that perfect blending of hearts and minds that a child would be allowed to bless the union.

The Mother left them to discover on their own, as they did rather quickly, that she had not restricted their mates to their own species.

Vampire and Werewolf kind were in an uproar. Most still

believed that humans were beneath them, and their guardian brethren were now a hated enemy. How could they mate outside of their culture?

Many prayed ceaselessly to the goddess to retract her conditions, but she refused to aid them any further.

They were all on their own."

"Doesn't seem like anyone's learned the Mother's lesson does it?" Zander looked down at Regina's quiet words and grimaced.

"They tried. Once they realized what she wanted them to do, many Weres and Vampires embraced their new path. But our goddess tested us. Mating the most sought-after *Were* females with the least receptive of our kind. Matching weak-minded humans, who couldn't adapt to their new abilities, with our strong-willed female Vampires. And then there were the 'accidents'."

"Accidents?"

"Just like humans, our kind has been known to mistake lust or infatuation for love. A member of ours or the Were species can be fairly intense in such a situation. If those feelings aren't returned by the one we believe to be our mate, well..."

"Let me guess. The first Unborn was created in one of these 'accidents'?" Zander flinched visibly at her sarcastic tone.

He nodded. "Exactly. A true mate is changed by Unity. A human would evolve into a *Were* or Vampire of similar abilities and genetics as their mate. An Unborn has been turned, but without the true joining of the soul and the blood, they are far more vulnerable than they would be mated to one who was born into our species."

"But Truebloods don't mate outside of their species."

117

"They used to. All the families in the thirteen Vampire clans have traces of human and or *Were* in their DNA."

Regina sat as far away from him as his arms allowed. "I know this. Every family but one."

Zander refused to let her look away, "Yes, every family but one. The Sariel's mates have always been other natural-born Vampires. It's the reason our family has held the position of Mediator to the Trust for generations."

All of her insecurities bubbled up to the surface at those words.

As a Gypsy, she recalled the *gaja*, or non-Gypsy prejudice against her kind. Her father had hated her and her mother's family because of their special abilities. Now, as an Unborn, not only was she once again kept on the edge of society, but she would be unable to be with Zander because of it. Suddenly his avoidance of her made sense.

Zander set her angrily off his lap, his stride irate as he crossed the room. She fell back against the far end of the sofa, her eyes wide.

He turned, pointing at her, before clenching his teeth and turning away once more. After a moment he faced her again, his long legs making quick work of the distance between them as he fell to his knees.

"Look into my mind, Regina. You *are* my mate. My gift from the Mother and my reason for living. I am sorry that others hurt you and betrayed you. Sorry others have taken away your ability to choose your own path. *That* is why I stayed away. I wanted to give you the chance to leave before I was unable to let you go."

Lux had told her as much. She knew they were mates. But how could he make such a choice? His line would be corrupted. The heads of the clans, the ones who made the rules of

118

separation in the first place, would be furious.

"The rules are wrong, Regina. My family has always been against it. Not only because it goes against the Mother's wishes, but because we have watched our people die off, one by one, without enough offspring to replenish their lines. We're a dying breed."

He dropped his forehead in her lap, breathing her in, as if being near her soothed him. "But even if the line of Mediators dies with me, even if our world as we know it crashes down around our ears because of it, I would not regret one single thing if only you were mine."

She placed her hand on his bowed head, her heart melting at his whispered confession. She felt his sincerity. He meant every word. Zander loved her.

Her fingers sifted through his short, sandy hair and marveled at the joy welling up within her. He had given her a choice. This strong-willed man, who was used to obedience and respect from Vampires and Weres alike, was actually in agony as he waited for her response. Did he truly believe she would turn him down?

There really was no choice to make. Her heart had decided the moment she'd woken up with him beside her. It had just taken a while for her mind to catch up. She lifted his head and looked down with a smile. Sapphire flared to life in his eyes as he pressed his lips softly against her own.

She felt the heat from his kiss coursing through her body, reawakening her earlier arousal as she pressed closer, parting her lips to allow his questing tongue entrance. This was where she belonged.

"Regina, my grathita, I have to tell you...have to ask you—"

But she knew. From what Lux had told her and what she'd been sensing from Zander, she knew what Unity entailed.

119

When Elizabeth had changed her, she had been bitten and then coerced into drinking of her sire's blood three times. It was an experience she barely remembered because of the thrall's effect on humans, but she'd seen it done many times since then.

According to Lux, Unity was similar. Three times they would have to share in each other's life force, drinking as one.

The first time had occurred quite by accident, when he'd been drawn to drink from her as his own blood healed her. This last time would merge them completely in a marriage of spirit, mind and body. Still Regina and Zander, but more. Their lives and their deaths would be inextricably joined. It was a little overwhelming, the trust involved in such a merger, but she knew it would be worth it.

Zander monitored her thoughts as their sweet embrace went on. He couldn't mask his elation, he'd been so sure she would argue, or be too frightened to go through with it.

They'd had a taste and he'd been raised knowing how Unity would change him, but neither could completely prepare for such an intimate joining. And as an Unborn, Regina would have to endure the physical transformation as well, though it would be nowhere near as traumatic as it would be for a mere human woman.

"Stop worrying. I want this. I want to be with you."

He slid his hands beneath her legs and drew her up into his arms. Carrying her to the bed they'd both missed sharing for days, he looked into her glowing golden eyes, his own shining with tenderness. "Far be it for me to deny my *grathita* anything she desires."

Chapter Seven

Zander couldn't take his eyes from Regina. He stood her on her feet beside the bed, feeling oddly tentative. He wanted this to be special for her. She was so beautiful, so important to him, he felt honored and humbled that she wanted to be his.

She backed up onto the bed, kneeling on the mattress before him, her body flushed with excitement, her eyes bright. Her fingers reached for the zipper of his slacks, hesitating.

She glanced up coyly from beneath her lashes. "I don't think I can wait to see you. Do you think you could...?" She blushed, but Zander understood.

A breathless gasp later, their clothes were gone, and she had her soft, slender fingers wrapped around his rapidly growing erection. He let out a shuddery groan and slid one trembling hand in her hair as she touched him.

Three days had been an eternity. He wanted to dive into her and drown in sensation. He wanted to take her hard and fast, again and again until they were both so sated they wouldn't be able to leave the bed for a week.

His hands clenched in the ebony strands of her hair as her lips wrapped around his pulsing arousal. She drew him deeply into her mouth, her joy at being this close to him again a palpable presence in the room.

She cared for him. And he knew now that when Regina's heart was involved, she would risk anything, even death, to protect the people she cared about. She was an amazing woman.

Mother Goddess, how he loved her.

His thoughts scattered at the feel of her hot mouth on his cock, hips arching against her instinctively as her tongue lashed the sensitive tip, swirling around the length of his shaft before wrapping her lips tight around him to suckle strongly once more.

"Your mouth feels so good, my love. Yes. Oh, priya, *if you don't stop soon I'm going to come."*

She increased her efforts at his words, and he felt the warning sparks, an electrical current that ran down his spine, signaling the coming explosion.

Helpless, Zander pumped his hips faster, his rock-hard erection disappearing down her throat as he fucked her mouth, praying to the Goddess that he wasn't hurting her. Unable to stop. He heard her moan, her pleasure clear in his mind and he could take no more.

Reggie was on fire.

She felt the waves of his climax echo through her body as he came with a roar in her mouth, the hot, salty taste inciting her need. She couldn't get enough. She lapped up every drop until he jerked away with a shiver, pulling her head back and bending to take her mouth in a heated kiss.

Their tongues warred, and she heard him groan in satisfaction at his taste in her mouth. The lash of his need burned through her, twining with her own, and she was lost.

The searing flesh of her back hit the cool comforter as he

pressed her down, pulling her legs to the edge of the bed and kneeling between them with a lusty groan.

There was no gentle, tentative teasing as his fingers spread her sodden folds, thrusting his tongue deep, rooting for more of her taste as if he were starving for her.

"I always hunger for you. I will never get enough of my grathita. Never."

Ablaze with sensation, her skin tingling with desire, she clutched the blanket beneath her as Zander continued to gorge himself on her taste. He was wild, his passion pulsing through her veins, elevating her need until she was sobbing with it.

She felt a pinch of pain as his sharp fangs nipped her soft, pink flesh, his lust and hers elevating as he tongued the small wound, gathering the tiny drops of blood along with her juices.

He stood and she moaned in denial at the loss. She opened her eyes and looked into his, his pupils so dilated his eyes appeared black, fangs extended and jaw tight with lust.

She wasn't afraid. She knew she looked just as wild. She longed for it, craved him in a way she had never imagined.

His gaze lit on her lips, tender and swollen from their lovemaking, her breasts, trembling with each panting breath, his chest rumbling with a needy growl at the sight.

Pulling her legs up over his shoulders, he aligned his arousal, once more hard with need, and drove deep. Her back arched off the bed, and she cried out at the completeness of the invasion. So perfect. They fit together so perfectly.

He leaned forward until her knees bent, gripping her breasts with rough palms, pinching her nipples with his fingers as he powered into her, hard and fast and impossibly deep. She strained her neck to kiss him, nipping his lips, arching into his caressing hands for more.

"*Do you accept me? Are you truly mine, Regina?*"

"*Yes! Yes, Zander. I am yours.*"

He lowered her legs to wrap them around his hips and pressed his chest to hers. She felt herself gathered on the edge, her entire being quivering with desire, her heart so full she was afraid it might burst from her chest. And then he smiled.

"*As one, my love, my* priya. *For all eternity and longer.*"

"*As one.*"

Her sharpened incisors cut smoothly through her gums and she bit down on his shoulder. He called her name aloud, before dipping his head to pierce her throat. She embraced him, drinking the blood from his veins while he thrust inside her. Then something began to happen.

What had been the tentative breeze of awareness in her consciousness became a storm. She had thought she'd felt him before, known him before, but this was so much more.

Time seemed to slow as the essence, the soul, all that he was joined with her, all his memories, hopes and dreams became hers as well. *Unity.*

In her mind she saw his childhood, the loving family that supported him. She saw him as a young man, his admiration and deep friendship for the older warrior Malcolm Abbadon, his pain at his hero's death.

The mantle of responsibility he'd been burdened with from birth, the knowledge that he would keep the balance of his world intact, his pride and acceptance. All of it was laid bare for her to see. Finally, she understood how much he loved her, that he was willing, without batting an eye, to turn his back on the sacred and honorable role his family had held since the inception of the Trust. That he was willing to sacrifice it all...for her.

The love and acceptance she had always craved dwelt within Zander's heart.

She came abruptly back to her body as the blasting waves of orgasm crashed down around her. Explosive bliss that rocked her to her core as tears of joy and satisfaction coursed her cheeks. It seemed to go on and on, Zander's climax bringing them together once more in a union that defied description.

At last. She was home. She licked his shoulder, lapping every drop of blood from his flesh as he did the same. He collapsed on top of her, but she welcomed his weight, welcomed the feel of him joined with her in every way possible. He was hers. And she was his *grathita.*

She thanked the Goddess of his people for bringing them together. If she had indeed been the one responsible for creating this blissful connection, Reggie would pray at her altar for all time.

All the pain and emotional scars, all the rejection she'd suffered, wiped away in one moment of time. She'd never felt so free. Never felt so alive.

Even as that thought formed the liquid, boneless warmth that filled her began to chill within her veins, and her heart took on a rapid irregular rhythm.

Zander lifted his head quickly, searching her eyes. She knew she looked confused. What was happening? It was as if she were encased in freezing water, water that was swiftly rising above her head.

"Zander?"

"Regina, my love, don't be afraid. It's part of the transformation process." But she didn't remember Lux or Zander telling her anything about this. And he seemed just as worried as she was. She tried to reach out mentally, to discover what was happening, but the ice that numbed her limbs had robbed her of her abilities.

"I'm here for you, my priya, *my* grathita. *I will never leave you. Rest now, Regina, when you wake, we will be together."*

She fought desperately to regain control of her body. Regardless of his assertions, she was sure she was, after all, actually going to die.

She had been content with that fate only a few days before, before she met Zander. Now when she'd finally found him, it was too late. Zander's voice assuring her, comforting her, was the last thing she heard before she lost consciousness.

Zander ran a shaking hand through his hair as he looked at his mate.

Pale and drawn, she lay still as a statue. Her breath was slow and shallow, frightening him half out of his mind.

For the first time since she'd arrived and he'd tasted her blood, Zander couldn't feel her. Not a whisper, not a flutter in his thoughts, not one single emotion. Even when she'd blocked him, he felt it like a wall with her unique signature in his mind. Never this void.

He paced the edge of the bed, wiping the cold sweat from his face as he gazed at her, willing her to move. *This is perfectly natural.* She was just in the sleep that Unborns and humans went through during the transformation. Why didn't that thought comfort him?

Truebloods hardly felt the change. They spent their Unity afterglow connected with each other, making love until the dawn. But the effect on those not natural-born was more intense, a change at the cellular level.

It was not unusual for them to fall into a deep sleep, similar to a coma as their bodies adapted. It was up to the

Trueblood mate to watch over his *grathita*, keeping her safe until she woke once more.

Zander had no frame of reference. He knew the basic facts—he'd had to learn every facet of his people's law and lore as Mediator. But none of his family, not one of them, had ever had to deal with this, this *absence* of their mate.

The withdrawal, and that was indeed what it was, after feeling such union, such completion was so painfully wrong to him that he wasn't sure if he could stand it.

As insane as it sounded, the desperation inside of him almost made him wish he could take it back. Take back the bonding and just keep her by his side, intact and joined with him, even if it was only a partial connection.

Regina? Regina, my love, please.

A swift knock on his door had him crouching protectively in front of the bed, a snarl on his lips as his fangs extended menacingly, determined to protect his *grathita*.

The door opened and Lux walked in, his sharp gaze quickly evaluating the dangerous scene. He approached his brother slowly, hands raised and head tilted down in a gesture of submission. "Zander, my brother, we must leave Haven at once."

A feral sound rumbled in Zander's throat. He knew his brother would never hurt Regina, but he was too close to where she lay. He must protect her. He would kill any who attempted to get by him. Rip out the throat of any who dared—

"Zander Sariel! I do *not* want your mate. We are all in danger and we must leave *now*."

Zander tilted his head, the red haze receding from his eyes as he took in his brother's serious expression. "What has happened?" His voice, rough with warning, was sane enough that Lux's shoulders slumped in relief.

"We need to get Reggie and the others to safety as soon as possible. Haven is under attack." Zander shook his head in confusion as an instinctive rage filled him at the words.

Lux continued, his tone low and intense as he attempted to reach his brother. "I was escorting my guest downstairs to her car, but when I got to the hallway door, I felt it. Someone has broken through our defenses... Haven is on *fire*. A fire that we can't put out."

He was trying to comprehend this shocking revelation. What was Lux trying to say? Not only was Haven equipped with a sprinkler system, but as a Vampire, with control over the elements, his brother should have been able to douse it with ease.

A fire that wouldn't die? A tingle of alarm spread down his spine as he realized he was once more witnessing the work of black magick, which could only mean one thing. "Shadow Wolf."

Lux nodded quickly as he backed towards the door. "Exactly. I believe Grey Wolf is attempting to force us to leave Haven. He must have had help to work this spell, someone who was able to enter unnoticed. He can't get in, otherwise he wouldn't be attempting to smoke us out. He's here for Regina and we must get her to safety."

Zander turned to scoop Regina up from the bed, her seemingly lifeless form causing him to shudder with concern. Wrapped up in his comforter, she lay limp in his arms and he turned towards the door to look at his brother, agony robbing his breath.

"She lives brother, you know this. It's the sleep. The sooner we get her to safety, the sooner she will wake and be with you once more."

Lux backed up quickly, ensuring there was enough room between him and his brother's parcel, painfully aware of

Zander's primitive need to keep others at bay.

In the hall at the top of the stairs, a worried Joel and a terrified human woman stood waiting. Zander bared his teeth. *Too close.*

Lux stepped in front of them, speaking in a low whisper. "Stay away from them both, and whatever you do, don't look at Regina."

He glanced at the paling Joel. "She's in the sleep. You've heard of a mate's protective instincts during Unity sleep." Joel nodded sharply.

"Just follow me."

Zander impatiently pressed past them, keeping his back to them and his *grathita* out of touching distance as he headed down the stairs.

He must get her to safety.

As he reached the foot of the stairs he could feel it, the unnatural heat of the fire. Haven had stood in one form or another for thousands of years. Never in all that time had anyone dared to breach its walls with intent to do harm.

A long thin tapestry hung to his right, threadbare and faded with time. He swept it aside without thought, finding the sliding panel that led to the pantry in the kitchen. He opened the pantry door wide, seeing the guardsmen standing nearby, waiting for Lux to return.

These were warriors, men whom his family had trusted for generations, trained to protect the reigning Mediator and his family from harm.

Zander and Lux had both trained with these fighters, learning the art of battle as children. They and those before them lived in secret, accountable only to the Sariel family, appearing only when danger threatened their charges. That they were here now could only bode ill. And if they didn't stop staring at his mate he would—

"Max. Kit." Lux cut a wide swath around his menacing brother and stepped towards the family guardsmen. "We need to get to the ruins. Quickly."

He blocked their view as they tried to look at the body in Zander's arms. "I wouldn't if I were you, gentlemen. He's newly mated."

Two sets of black eyes widened, and they both nodded before turning and heading towards the larder door hidden beneath a crate on the floor. Dust floated in the air as the door creaked and lifted, revealing a spiral staircase leading below ground.

Zander held tight to Regina as he followed the men who towered even over him down the dark escape route. No one but the Sariels and a few trusted allies knew this existed. The Shadow would expect to see the brothers running from Haven unprepared. They were foolish.

Even before the war with the Loups De L'Ombre, the Sariels had known their position and authority might fuel the fire of resentment. The protections the Healers had placed in the air around the pub was like a silent alarm to them, one that for some reason hadn't warned them of the coming danger. This escape route was their last resort.

Zander barely noticed the trek as they walked through the tunnel of reinforced brick and concrete. The torches that lined the walls lit with the spark of their minds as they moved swift and silent.

His only thought was Regina. He stared down at his mate. He clung to the memories of the Unity experience, how he'd merged with all that she was. How beautiful her soul seemed to him. And though he'd gleaned bits and pieces of her story, he hadn't seen the whole picture until tonight.

The most disturbing point had been when he'd realized what she'd planned to do after informing his family of the danger to her clan. The thought that he might have lost her if he hadn't tasted of her blood, realized she was his. The idea that this courageous spirit even considered taking her own life, stepping into the dawn that was certain death to all Unborns.

She believed she was of no use. That her power had brought her nothing but heartbreak, been useless to her clan. That it was the reason Grey Wolf had become more determined than ever to destroy everything she cared about.

His mate had no idea how powerful she was. But he knew now. He understood so many things. And seeing her Daj Mia through her mind, "remembering" her stories and legends, the ones that so closely resembled those he'd heard on his mother Nya's knee, as well as those Lux had shared from his studies with Glynn Magriel, he realized how important she was to Vampirekind.

Regina was the bravest being he had ever known. Braver than the warriors he'd admired as a child. Braver than he'd ever had to be. And he loved her with an intensity that shook him to his soul. He would spend a thousand lifetimes proving it to her...as soon as she woke up.

They walked for what felt like days. Zander looked back to see the sleeping human cradled in Lux's arms, Joel following close behind.

Finally, he saw the giant steel door ahead. The door that meant safety for his mate. The family safe-house, the Sariels' own personal sanctuary.

Kit stood to one side as Max keyed in the code on the alarm hidden by a false brick in the wall. The door slid open, slow and silent, revealing a well-lit foyer, complete with marble floor and a chandelier dangling from the ceiling.

"Ruins?" Zander heard Joel whisper to his brother. Lux chuckled softly.

"The ruins of a castle that was built above us years ago. The way out brings us directly to them."

Their home beneath the ruins was built for comfort. Zander's mother had redecorated ages past, making sure that should they ever need a place to "hide out", it would be done in lavish style. There was a game room, a den, five luxurious bedrooms, three full baths and a kitchen full of non-perishables.

Zander headed directly to his room, passing the guards and leaving his brother to deal with the hosting duties. His room was a near-duplicate of the one back at Haven. He was nothing if not consistent. Although since Regina, his usual routine had been thoroughly shaken up.

The only glaring difference was a built-in Jacuzzi where the kitchenette should have been. It sat in the floor, surrounded by marble tiles, and Zander didn't hesitate. Laying his fragile bundle on the bed, he turned the jets on and raised the temperature before flashing out of his dusty clothes.

Removing the comforter and carrying her cold, bare form to the water's edge, he sank into the shallow pool, Regina safely in his embrace. He rubbed her arms and hands gently, holding her close to his heart as if he could somehow transfer his warmth to her.

He couldn't think about the pub, couldn't think about the enemy outside when his mind was filled with this longing to touch hers. She was the only thing that mattered. He didn't think he could stand it, even for a single night.

When he felt the lethargy-inducing combination of the heated jets and the rising of the sun, he carried them both to bed.

Leaning against the headboard, Zander rocked her in his arms, telling her of this place he'd brought them, of his love for her. Begging her, until he could no longer fight his exhaustion, to come back to him.

Chapter Eight

This wasn't Haven. Reggie wasn't sure how she knew, but she woke with the knowledge clear in her mind. Her eyes remained closed, thoughts fuzzy as she took stock of the feelings and images swirling around in her head.

"Brother, you must drink. If not for yourself, think of your *grathita*. When she wakes she'll need nourishment, and you've had nothing for two days." It was Lux.

Two days? Had she really been asleep for two days? And then she remembered.

Unity.

She had been filled with joy and satisfaction, but that warmth was quickly overtaken by icy fear and blackness. And then she'd begun to dream.

She'd dreamt of the moon, the beautiful moon glowing with love and compassion—like a goddess in the sky. And fire. She thought she might have spoken to her Daj Mia but she couldn't be sure. There were too many images, too many feelings—hers and Zander's—bombarding her, confusing her.

There was a shocked silence, followed by a wave of love and relief so strong it almost brought her to tears. She lifted her heavy lids as the bed dipped beside her. Zander brushed a shaking hand against her cheek, cupping it as he leaned close to look into her eyes.

"My priya. *Regina. Welcome back, my love."*

He looked worse than she felt. His face was filled with tired shadows, his cheeks sunken and pale. But it was his eyes, burning with a sapphire fire and wet with unshed tears that held her captive.

"I missed you, Regina mine. You must never leave me again. How do you feel?"

She reached up to touch his face, her concern for him putting her own minor aches and disorientation on the back burner. He needed to feed, that much was clear. Had he stayed beside her this entire time?

"Where else would I be? Don't worry, I'm just fine."

"Lux." Her throat was dry, her voice gravelly with sleep. She heard a swift, shuffling noise and then he was there, his burgundy hair pulled back in a slick queue, his expression tight with concern though he tried to smile as he looked down at her from over Zander's shoulder.

"He needs blood. You brought Molly?" Lux laughed and shook his head ruefully at her question.

"I know I shouldn't be surprised anymore, but having a sister-in-law with your abilities is a little disconcerting."

"Well, I can't morph or zap clothes away with a glance...yet. So we're even." She licked her dry lips, swallowing a whimper as she attempted to sit upright.

Zander reached out his arms to help her, but she stopped him with a shake of her head, her hand on his chest. "You need to feed, Zander."

His shoulders tensed and he shrugged, watching her sluggish movements with an alert eye. "There's synth-blood in the kitchen, as soon as you're better I'll—"

"Synth-blood isn't going to cut it, brother. Not after all this time without. You've barely slept, you haven't eaten and you need to be at your full strength for tonight."

As she listened to Lux lecture Zander, her stomach jumped to her throat. Tonight. The Clan Trust was tonight. She would have to face the leaders of all the Trueblood clans.

Her stomach fluttered nervously, but she tried to push it out of her mind. Zander needed her. That was all that mattered. And she wasn't about to let him face those dragons in a weakened condition.

She sent a silent request to the human woman who sat quiet as a mouse on the other side of the room. Zander's blue eyes flashed in surprised warning as he realized what she was doing.

When Molly joined the small gathering at the edge of the bed and held out her arm to him, he glanced at it in momentary disgust before catching Reggie's reproving glance.

She could sense his train of thought. It was too soon after Unity, too soon since he'd lost his connection to her, been sure she would die and he along with her. He understood that he needed sustenance, but another woman? He hesitated. She knew immediately what she had to do.

"Zander, my mate. Take what she offers so freely. Take it...and then take me."

She watched his jaw clench with desire as he inhaled deeply, seeking control. This new connection between them was so intensely intimate it was hard to tell whose feelings were whose, whose memories filled her mind.

Images of their joining a few days before, of Zander taking her, hard and fast and uncaring of their audience, whipped through her, filling her body with liquid fire.

He gently grasped Molly's waiting arm, pulling it closer to his mouth, his eyes never leaving Reggie's. His fangs extended and she felt the slide of her own as he bit down into the pale, trembling flesh.

She could smell the woman's blood, could hear her heart pounding its erratic drum beat, could sense Zander's hunger matching her own.

He never blinked. Never once took his eyes, so filled with blue promise, from her enraptured gaze. It was unbearably erotic.

He seemed to grow stronger, his skin flushing with health, his eyes sparkling with passion. Reggie couldn't catch her breath, her need for him growing with each passing moment.

She became achingly aware of her nudity beneath the comforter, her legs shifting restlessly as she waited for him to drink his fill. She felt no jealousy. She knew he belonged to her. And she wanted him.

Now.

Zander's lashes fluttered as he licked the moaning woman's arm, her body leaning against Lux as he crooned his encouragement. Reggie looked on as her mate patted the woman's hand in thanks before standing abruptly.

"Leave us." His voice, low and harsh with lust, echoed commandingly through the room.

Reggie looked over at the couple as they hurried to comply. Lux winked at her, a thank-you forming on his silent lips as he rushed the aroused young human out the door. A shiver of excitement sent moisture pooling between her thighs as she turned her head to look back at her mate.

"You trust me." It was not a question, but Reggie answered anyway.

"How can I do anything else? You're a part of me."

Satisfaction blazed from him as he took a step closer, his

powerful thighs pressing against the bed, flexing with impatience. He opened a drawer on the table beside the bed, pulling out several strands of velvet ribbon. *"Trust me more."*

She didn't have time to question his mysterious order before she found herself being turned, her hands placed on the headboard and tied with the ribbon.

Her pulse raced as she realized what he intended to do. Her mind went back to that first time, when he'd imagined doing this to her, restraining her for his pleasure, torturing her with sensation until she begged for him. She hadn't been sure of him then, hadn't known him, joined with him. His fantasy was now her own. She wanted him to take her however he wanted, whenever he wanted.

"That's good to know, sweet priya. I've wanted this from the moment I saw you, bent and tied for me. Open to me, needing me so desperately you were dripping with it."

He slid his fingers through her arousal, gliding them slowly up until they pressed against the tight hole between her cheeks.

"I'm going to take you here, fill you so full and tight...you want that don't you, Regina mine?"

"Yes."

Yes, she wanted that with every cell in her body. She recalled the scene she'd witnessed a few nights before when Lux took Joel that way, so forceful, so primal and beautiful. On her knees she raised her hips, pressing into his hand in a silent plea for more.

"Soon, Regina. But first..."

She felt him move and then he was beneath her, on his back between her legs, hands tight on her ass as he lowered her to his waiting mouth. She hesitated, but he was determined.

Soon Reggie was writhing on him, crying out as he drank

her down in greedy gulps. His fingers returned once more to the tight, tempting ring of muscles and she felt them pushing inside, stretching her, readying her, his tongue thrusting aggressively inside her wet heat.

Reggie fisted her hands around the headboard, pulling lightly against her bonds, mindless with excitement. The twinge of fear and discomfort she'd been dreading at being tied this way, helpless, never came. Not even the nightmares of her past could stand between them and the pleasure he was giving her.

Her climax caught her unawares. She called out his name on a sob, pressing her sex against his mouth as he continued his voracious assault. When his name was an endless litany on her lips and in her mind, her clit swollen and sensitive from his attentions, he slid out from his prone position and knelt behind her.

"Are you ready, grathita? *Are you ready for me?"*

He knew she was. She felt his hard, bare cock pulse against her, before pressing slow and sure into her ass. She breathed deeply, the fullness unbelievable, the pain-pleasure so intense it brought tears to her eyes.

Electric shocks of sensation licked up her spine. He pushed through the resistance of her clinging muscles, groaning aloud, burying himself to the hilt inside her.

"Mother Goddess! So tight—so tight around my cock. Regina...my priya, oh yes!"

Her entire body was trembling with adrenaline and need. Thankful for the bonds and his tender grip that kept her from shattering into a million pieces.

He dragged his hips back, the tight fit causing them both to moan in ecstasy, before he thrust deep once more.

It was devastating, powerful. Their minds merged and focused, their senses so attuned to each other that it was

139

impossible to tell who took and who was taken. Soon he was driving deep and fast inside her, and she pressed back just as aggressively, flying in headlong desperation towards their goal.

"Now, Regina. Take what you need. Ahh, goddess, it feels so good.

He slid an arm around her chest, pulling her back until the velvet cloth tightened around her wrists, a thrill shooting through her at the sting. He placed his forearm against her lips, urging her to drink from him, to feed as she came.

She bit into him, the warm blood filling her mouth, renewing her, replenishing her as he continued to pump his hips against her. She felt her soul wrapped serenely around his, irrevocably joined, then the world tilted on its axis.

She flew further than she'd ever gone, came so hard that stars danced behind her lowered lids. He growled against her shoulder as he felt her clench her muscles around him, his cock pounding inside her as he came, his hot seed filling her, burning her.

Dazed and shivering as she came back to herself, she realized that he had already untied her bonds, was even now holding her close as he rubbed the soreness from her wrists.

They lay together on the bed until their stomachs rumbled. Zander called to have some food brought to his room while Reggie found the Jacuzzi.

Sitting together in the heated water, they ate some fresh fruit that Kit, the intimidating guard, had brought back from his quick excursion to the surface for reconnaissance. As they filled their bellies, they talked about what they'd both been through these last few days.

"I should be mad at you and Lux for not warning me about the sleep." The sting of her unspoken accusation was taken away as she slid her legs around his hips, floating beside him in the soothing, swirling waters, feeding him an orange wedge.

He wrapped his arms around her, accepting the tart offering with solemn eyes. "I had no real idea what would happen. I knew the basics, but I'd never seen—when you went so still, when I couldn't reach you, couldn't feel you in my mind..."

His eyes closed in remembered agony and he pulled her closer.

She soothed him, feeling his anguish and wanting only to wipe it away. "I had some pretty unusual dreams."

Zander pulled back, looking at her oddly. "I've never heard of any Unborn or human having dreams during the Unity sleep. It's a kind of coma the body goes into while the DNA alterations take effect, insuring fertility and compatibility with the Trueblood mate."

"Well *I* did. I dreamt of Daj Mia. She apologized for calling me an abomination, said she hadn't known. Then I saw a lot of confusing images. The full moon, a battle, Lux and Arygon...and you." She smiled up at him. "You saved me."

The hair stood up on the back of Zander's neck. The full moon was tonight.

As the images she was describing wavered in his mind through their connection, he couldn't help but wonder if it was an omen of some kind. And what had Lux been doing beside that Were Arygon?

She still had no inkling of her power, but it stood to reason it had also been enhanced along with the rest of her vampiric abilities.

The connection had been affecting him as well. He'd noticed while she was sleeping that he was able to catch some of the concerned thoughts Lux and the others had been sharing.

He hadn't had the energy to think about it, not when he'd been so focused on his sleeping bride. But now, he couldn't help the curiosity that filled him at the possible ramifications of mating with a Reader. How much of her abilities did he actually share?

More importantly, how much had she changed? His concern for the dangers to come had him pulling her out of the hot tub and into the middle of the room. "Dry yourself, Regina."

She looked at him as if he were insane, before shrugging and reaching for one of the towels they'd laid beside the small pool.

He reached out a hand to stop her. "No. Use the air in the room."

He felt her confusion and smiled his apology. "I keep forgetting how little you know about your own kind. You may have unique telepathic abilities, abilities we've forgotten, but we are not completely without power, as you know."

He stood and called the air, a blast of warmth surrounding him for an instant, and he was dry. Her eyes went wide and he felt her search his mind for instructions.

She closed her eyes and crinkled up her arched brows in concentration, making him smile. After a moment, he felt the air stir, followed by a blast of hot wind that almost knocked her tiny, nude frame to the floor.

He couldn't help but laugh as she glared at him from between her drying strands of ebony hair. "At least we know you *can* do it, now all you have to practice is control."

"Ya think?" She grumbled, but he could feel the excitement filling her mind as she considered the possibilities.

Her mouth opened on a gasp and she looked at him

sideways before she once again closed her eyes in concentration. Before he could stop her, he saw her skin begin to ripple. Energy shimmered around her as her body reformed. He went to open the closet door where a mirror waited, showing her what she had become.

"I can do it, Zander! After two hundred years I can change my shape!

I'm a bird? That's not remotely frightening. Liz can change into a panther, and Nicolette...well let me just tell you she's scary. I'd be lucky if I frightened a grasshopper in this form."

Zander smiled, he'd thought her a little raven when he'd first met her, and here she was, changed into a blackbird before his eyes. *"Ravens are powerful birds, Regina mine. They bring knowledge, foretell the future and more importantly, they can fly away from danger. I think you're beautiful."*

As she pruned her feathers, looking this way and that in the mirror, He grinned and began to shimmer.

The loud squawk she emitted when a giant golden bear appeared behind her was comical. In moments they had both changed back, Regina sprawled on the floor laughing. He came to sit beside her, entranced by her laughter.

As she wiped the tears of mirth from her eyes, he felt another ripple of worry. "If there is trouble tonight, I want you to get away anyway you can. Now that we know you can change form, you can fly back here and wait for me to return."

"Are you expecting something? Beyond the whole Clan Trust wanting me executed for being a Reader, that is."

Zander raised his eyebrow. Another side effect of Unity, he couldn't keep anything a secret. He shrugged slightly, still unsure himself of the concerns in his mind.

"Just promise me you'll be careful." She nodded, wrapping her arms around him and pulling him down on the floor. As she attempted to kiss his concerns away, he sent up a prayer to the Mother that he would be up to the coming challenge.

"Are we alone?" Lux looked up from the billiards table, nodding shortly before focusing on his aim once more.

Zander stepped into the game room, smiling as he glanced around at the only room in the safe house that his father had been allowed to decorate. One corner was crammed with books of every genre and time period and two overstuffed leather chairs, perfect for hours of literary comfort.

Another side of the room was a testament to his love of gadgets. Video games and machines piled on the floor, even one of those irritating robotic dogs sat patiently waiting to be turned on and given instructions. And since it couldn't be called a game room without a billiards table, they had one of those too, although Alexander Sariel had no inclination to play.

"Yes. I sent Joel to take little Molly home. Poor thing, she's had a rough couple of days." He sunk his final ball and put his cue away. Zander chuckled.

"I'm sure she'll decide it was worth it."

His brother had a decidedly lascivious glimmer in his eyes. "Yes. I do believe she will. And before you can ask, I put her in the thrall, so she correctly assumes she had a few days of ecstasy, but nothing more. And Joel...well he knows the punishment for leading anyone to our door."

"I had no doubt that you would handle it correctly." Zander watched as, after a few moments, Lux began to pace around the room like a caged animal. He was restless. "What troubles you, brother?"

Lux laughed and ran a hand through his long hair, leaning against the pool table and crossing his arms. "You mean besides the fact that we are taking your newly awakened Reader mate into a den of judgmental cows, Haven is a burnt shell of black magick mischief *and* we have a lunatic with unbelievable powers searching for us as we speak?"

He exhaled roughly. "Glynn visited me in a dreamwalk last night. She warned me of danger coming, and let me know she was coming to the Clan Trust gathering tonight. Something she has *never* done before. I'm worried about you, Zander. Worried for the both of you."

Zander stepped forward and pulled his brother into a strong embrace, humbled at his concern. The new information about Glynn Magriel's presence made him even more determined to protect his mate.

The Healer rarely left her commune, for any reason. And her warning of danger only emphasized Regina's dream, and his own concern. His mind leapt ahead to the meeting, all the possible outcomes, most of which were unacceptable to him. He needed insurance, and he needed it fast.

"Come on, Lux. We need to prepare. Whatever happens, we have to be ready."

"I think you'd look stunning in the gold. It would match your eyes to perfection."

Reggie whirled around with a gasp, stunned to see a petite woman with sandy curls smiling at her as she sat on the edge of the canopy bed.

Zander had led her into this room and told her that she could find something to wear in the closet. She'd just been wondering who these fabulous creations belonged to, when the woman appeared as if out of thin air.

"I'm...I'm sorry if this is your room. There was a fire and Zander said..." She blushed as she realized she was naked but for the small towel that barely closed around her. The woman

145

waved her hand in a dismissive gesture, hopping down from the high bed and over to where Reggie was shifting in awkward embarrassment.

"Don't worry, I understand. You need to have something to wear to the meeting tonight. Good clothing can be better than armor, especially with *those* shallow peacocks. Kit and Max told me about the fire when I arrived. That and a few other interesting tidbits of information."

Reggie looked over at the woman who was sifting through the hanging items in the closet, and her heart nearly stopped. This was Zander's mother. She recognized her from his memories. This was her...mother-in-law. Nya Sariel.

"Lady Nya, it's an honor to meet you." She attempted to curtsy, her state of undress making it an odd, ungainly bob as she grappled with the corners of the cloth. "Zander didn't tell me you were coming."

And he'd certainly get an earful about that, she thought, as she sent him a mental SOS.

Nya's eyes sparkled as they studied Reggie. A mischievious smile played at her lips. "We came back early from our travels. When I sensed that Zander had found his *grathita*, well, I had to meet you."

She looked Reggie over from head to toe, sapphire eyes widening as they lingered on the mark on her forehead. It was obvious from the thoughts Reggie was sensing that she realized what she was. Apart from a momentary jolt and a lingering worry for her son, she seemed to take it in stride.

Looking back towards the closet, she pulled out a very simple black one-piece pantsuit and handed it to Reggie. "I think this will look wonderful on you. You don't need anything to distract from your exotic features. Also, it's the perfect foil for this." Nya unhooked a necklace from around her neck. It was made entirely of small, circular garnets, with one large glittering stone in the center. She reached around Reggie and closed the clasp.

"This is the Sariel family talisman, it represents the purity of our life force, and it has been worn by every Mediator's mate since the first. It's tradition to pass it on to the mate of the eldest son.

She stepped back and smiled. "It looks wonderful on you."

Reggie was confused. How could Nya accept her so easily? How could she offer her, of all people, a symbol of the purity of the Sariels? Especially when her tainted blood would herald the end of that illustrious line?

"Because she's my mother and she wants my happiness above all things. Plus, she likes you...I can tell. That and she's been wanting grandchildren for the last three hundred years."

Reggie heard him a moment before he appeared through the open doorway. Placing a finger to his lips with a grin, he made a production out of sneaking stealthily behind his mother. An instant before he reached her, she turned to face him, and Reggie could see the strong family resemblance as they embraced.

"Zander Sariel, when will you learn that a mother has eyes in the back of her head?"

"Oh, gross." The two male voices, speaking in perfect unison, had Reggie clenching her towel tighter as Lux arrived. He picked their small, spunky mother up in his arms, twirling her as she laughed in delight.

Reggie stepped into the closet to dress, rolling her eyes, though she was secretly a little envious of their close family unit. She wished she had known her own mother. Wished she had those special, private jokes that all families share.

"We are your family now, Regina mine. And as soon as Lux

gets over his infatuation for you, I'm sure he and I will share many a joke at your expense."

She snorted, sending him evil thoughts as she zipped up the soft, skintight suit. One inch smaller and it wouldn't have fit. Nya was a very tiny woman. When she stepped out from behind a line of party gowns, the trio was standing silent, waiting for her to appear.

She did a turn and held out her arms, feeling unusually shy. "Will this do?"

Nya was beaming like a proud mother hen, but the men had a different reaction. Lux's cheeks had darkened slightly as if he were blushing.

And Zander? Well Zander was glaring again, which, she thought with an inward giggle, was a good sign.

"Mother, don't you think something a bit more...concealing would be appropriate for this interview?" Nya rolled her eyes at Reggie and she knew at that moment that she was going to love this woman.

She walked over to the mirror and was impressed with how sophisticated she looked. The jewels sparkled cool and dark around her neck. Standing out as Nya said they would against the classic black of her suit.

It was as elegant as Nicolette in style, the material silk and the lines sleek. It was also sexy and dangerous—a long sleeved one-piece outfit with a slight flare at the legs and a definite dip at the neckline. Liz would love it too.

Reggie decided then and there that she wanted a dozen of her own. It was her own personal version of her sire's "kick ass" fashion sense. It was amazing how confident she felt. Well, at least she would look her best at the execution.

"Don't even joke about that, Regina."

"I think Lux and I need to go speak to your father, Zander. You look wonderful, dear. Welcome to the family." Nya smiled at her once more before dragging a chuckling Lux out the door.

Zander came to stand behind her, sliding his arms around her waist until she leaned against him. As they stood together, the giant, beloved Mediator and the pint-sized Gypsy Unborn, she couldn't help thinking how perfectly they fit together. How fated and right.

"I couldn't agree more. And I couldn't be prouder than I am right now, seeing you wearing the proof of our blood-bond around your neck for all to see."

She worried the necklace with shaky fingers. "I thought you said you didn't want them to focus on our mating. That you wanted them to listen to my proof, and that they wouldn't if they thought we were together."

"I just spoke with my father and he agreed that you need more protection. The Sariels as an ally are formidable. As family, they are merciless. I want you safe, Regina. The Trust will listen to what we have to say. I guarantee it. The Deva Clan will be safe."

He instinctively understood her worry. She couldn't care less whether they accepted her, although it would certainly make her mate's life easier, but her duty to her clan was paramount. They had to be protected.

"*I swear to you, my* priya. *I swear to you they will be safe. We will make this work...together.*"

Chapter Nine

They were an arresting procession, the group of Vampires ascending the wrought-iron staircase to the surface, led by their stoic guard, dressed all in black.

Reggie held the soft wool cape that Nya had given her tighter, as much for emotional comfort as to ward off the coming cold.

What would the next few hours bring? She'd had no idea when she'd run from Grey Wolf's torture that she would end up here. Mated to one of the most prominent Truebloods in existence and heading to a secret Trust meeting as a Sariel, instead of an Unborn.

What would Liz say if she knew? She hated Truebloods. Nicolette held no loyalty to them either. So many of her clan had been brutalized or abandoned by their creators. Was she being disloyal to them now? By loving the enemy?

"You know I can hear what you're thinking, right?"

She laughed quietly and reached behind her to grasp Zander's hand. She wouldn't change an instant of her time with her mate. Everything that she was, heart and soul, belonged to him now. But she owed the Devas so much. And she worried about their reaction.

"If they love you, they will understand. And Liz doesn't hate all Truebloods. Think of Lux. Of her husband Malcolm.

"*She just hates hypocrisy, whatever form it comes in. As long as you're happy, she'll be happy for you. I know it. Who knows, maybe she'll calm down and stop causing so much chaos now that you're one of us.*"

Though she doubted it, the thought temporarily soothed her. As they reached the surface, Max entered the code to open a hatch camouflaged to resemble a fallen building stone on the ground, and Reggie took a deep breath. It was almost time.

Five guards stood silent watch at the opening, all of them just as massive as Kit and Max. They wore the same old-style leather armor, their stoic gazes alert.

Their faces appeared etched in hard marble, stunning and powerful. They were the kind of warriors you read about, but never thought to see in real life. Curiously, Kit was not among them.

Zander had told her about the guards. None of the other Trueblood families knew their origins, although their unique abilities were renowned. Not Truebloods, not Unborns...but something completely different. And whatever *it* was, it caused no end of speculation among the clan houses that knew of their existence.

They didn't shift into animals. Instead, when the Sariel guards morphed, it was in sheer size and strength that they changed. Their presence struck fear in the hearts of all who were forced to face them. With their black, fathomless eyes, swift silence and unparalleled fighting abilities, they could have reigned over the Truebloods and Weres alike.

Instead they were the loyal, unshakeable protectors of Zander's family. Her mate had told her that one of his ancestors had saved theirs, and inducted them into the Sariel Clan. In return for that and some land on the outskirts of his clan's property, they trained their children for service as Sariel guards.

They were giants on the earth. Regina could only be thankful that they were on her side tonight.

One of them walked up to Zander, speaking in hushed tones. She watched his face hardening in controlled rage as he listened to the guard's words.

He caught her eye, coming up beside her and facing his family with the news. "The knowledge of Haven's destruction has spread. One particular council member and his heir apparent are demanding that we hold the Trust meeting within *their* walls. They have claimed that only there can the safety of all concerned be assured, since the Sariels seem unable to do their job as proprietors of sanctuary."

His mother Nya gasped and clung to her husband. Alexander Sariel, a near replica of his eldest son, grew still at the insult. "They go too far."

Reggie didn't have to ask who they were referring to. The Abbadons. Sebastian and his family had obviously decided to go on the offensive. Did they suspect that Reggie knew about their traitorous activities? Or were they just offended by her presence?

"I think it has more to do with me than you, *grathita*." Zander lowered his head to speak softly as they continued their trek through the snow-covered hills in the direction of the Abbadon estate. "Sebastian has always disliked the fact that my opinion holds more sway with the Trust than his. He would love nothing more than to take that influence away for good."

And now he had his reason. Reggie knew he would use her status as an Unborn to undermine Zander's authority. And when he discovered she was no longer of the lower caste, that she was now, in fact, Zander's mate? She could only imagine how much he would enjoy using that in his favor.

"Do not worry about Abbadon. We'll say what we must to warn the Trust and deal with what comes. All you have to think about is what I plan to do to you when I get you home."

And just like that she was breathless with need and anticipation. Gone were the six warriors positioned around them, hiding between the shafts of moonlight with a grace and stealth that was without equal. Gone were the rest of the Sariels and her worries about the coming meeting. All she saw, all she knew, was Zander.

How could he do this to her so swiftly? Take away her control. Make her long for his touch.

"I am yours, grathita, and you are mine. We will always feel this way for each other."

He kept her distracted with sensual words and images until they arrived at the imposing gates of Abbadon Keep. Their guards had stopped just over the last rise, ready should they be needed.

She was trembling beside him, though not in fear, and it was gratifying to know he was no better off. Her smirk was smug as they passed the expressionless sentinels at the gate.

"Welcome Sariels...Regina." Sebastian stood in the open doorway of his home, his arms spread in greeting.

He bowed his head formally, allowing the others past. His hand shot out suddenly, grasping Reggie by the arm before she could enter.

Sebastian's eyes narrowed to mere slits, honing in immediately on the gleaming red jewels draped around her neck. His grip was bruising, and Zander growled low, wrapping his larger fist around the dandy's thin wrist.

"I would take your hand off *my mate*, Abbadon. Unless you

want to lose it."

Reggie shivered. She felt the oily satisfaction oozing off their host. He released her arm with a shrug, backing away, letting Zander guide her quickly into the great hall beyond.

She smiled away the looks of worry coming from Nya and Alexander, walking close beside Lux and Zander as they were led towards the meeting room.

Abbadon Keep was the height of ostentation. Dramatic and showy—a little like Sebastian himself. It glittered with priceless paintings in frames of pure gold.

A large mural of cherubs being devoured by dark, fanged angels hung menacingly over their heads. Psychotic and twisted sculptures depicting Vampires draining ecstatic, nubile victims lined the halls, causing Reggie's stomach to churn with bile. So it wasn't cheesy Vampire novels that had made Abbadon the way he was after all, perhaps it simply ran in the family.

They entered the meeting area. A crowd had already assembled, lining the walls, the circular table in the middle of the room, the Trust members seated with somber expressions around it, at the center of everyone's attention.

It was the right of any Trueblood to witness the proceedings of their governing body, and approach them with any issues and concerns pertaining to their laws.

It was obvious from Nya's surprised inhalation and a few of the more prevalent thoughts Reggie was catching from around the room, that there hadn't been this many observers since the war. The thought didn't fill her with confidence. It seemed everyone wanted to see what she had to say that was important enough to call this emergency session.

"Grathita. *I want you to remain silent, no matter what you hear, until I call you to bear witness. But don't think I won't need your help...your talents. Knowing which way the wind is blowing* has never been more important than it is tonight. Will you help me?"

Reggie agreed mutely. Though a part of her was afraid of what she might find, she'd utilize every skill she had to make sure Zander had what he needed. They couldn't afford to miss a thing. Too much was at stake.

She studied the prestigious gathering of the twelve heads of the trueblood clans seated around the dark mahogany table, their proud expressionless faces barely acknowledging the Sariels' arrival.

Zander went to stand before them, directly in front of the floor-to-ceiling painting that depicted an important battle in the Vampires' war with the Shadow Wolves. The Abbadon warriors stood out in stark relief, their red and gold banners waving proudly as they fought their way through the partially shifted *Were* sorcerers.

Storms lashed across the sky of the canvas, drawn down by the hand of the most detailed and eye-catching figure in the painting. Malcolm Abbadon, she realized. He was young in this painting, but powerful. That it paid homage to his heroics was not in question. The Abbadon family was exceedingly proud of their martyred hero, and holding the Trust meeting here was the clearest way to remind everyone of their importance in the community.

Her mate bowed his head in a show of respect to the Trust members, meeting the eyes of each one of them, including Sebastian. The younger man had slid into the seat behind his father, an indication that he would soon hold his place in the Trust.

Zander held up a hand to silence the mutterings of their audience.

"In the name of the Mother Goddess, in perfect trust we

come. With honor and honesty, clear intent and wisdom we come. As we have since we allied as one, since before recorded time, we gather with a single goal, the good of our people."

A chorus of agreement echoed around the table, and the senior Abbadon, his skeletal features a harsh reflection of his son's, stood and asked for acknowledgement before he spoke to the room at large.

"Mediator Sariel. You have called us without warning, by right of *Tarjana*. What threat is so imminent that you bring The Clan Trust together before our scheduled time? Let us resolve this teapot tempest quickly, that we may address matters of greater import. Specifically, a discovery made by my heir, Sebastian Abbadon. One that will change all of our lives for the better."

The muttering of the crowd resumed, distracting Reggie as she attempted to discern the jumbled, near-maniacal thoughts of the older Abbadon.

He believed Sebastian would bring him fame beyond that of his deceased firstborn, Malcolm. He believed the Abbadons would become the saviors of Vampirekind, and he the patriarch worshipped by all.

When she tried to establish just what he was so excited about, a fog appeared, as if the cloud were in his mind. It almost seemed as if he were as in the dark about his son's plans as she was, but that didn't make any sense.

"Elder Abbadon, there is no doubt we are all anxious to hear about this amazing discovery. However, I believe that the Mediator would not have called us here unless the reasons were most dire. Mediator, would this threat have anything to do with the recent fire at Haven? And the Unborn beside you, while lovely, is a breach in protocol that I think we must have an explanation for."

She paled as every eye in the room turned her way. She had kept the shawl on, and after the incident with Sebastian, decided to use it to cover the Sariel heirloom, at least until it was time for it to be revealed.

She felt the discomfort, the disgust and...sympathy? Yes, the man who had spoken, one of the Elders, held none of the animosity for Unborns the others did. Serene in his royal blue colors and shock-white hair, he smiled kindly at her before looking towards Zander in query.

"Thank you, Elder Meroth, for your confidence. And in answer to your question—yes, the fire at Haven was directly related to the threat I have brought us here to address. As to Regina, she was the actual target of the unnatural blaze, because of the information she has that a certain Were and his cohorts do not want her to share."

"We have no disagreement with any Were pack, Mediator Sariel. What information could be so important that sanctuary would be threatened? No one would be fool enough." This from a rather pompous-looking woman in violet robes.

"Under normal circumstances, Elder Magriel, that would be true. But this is not a normal Were. This is a Shadow, a survivor of the Loups De L'Ombre. And as you know, there is only one way a dark sorcerer could breach our barriers."

The room erupted in chaos as everyone began talking at once. Shadow Wolves? But hadn't they all been destroyed centuries ago? And what had the Mediator meant by that last remark? Was he suggesting that they had a traitor in their midst?

The pompous Elder Magriel, obviously a relation of Lux's teacher Glynn, had gone eerily grey, seeming to shrink in her chair at the mere mention of the monsters that had terrorized her people so many years before.

She felt a rush of panic moments before Sebastian pushed back his chair abruptly, pushing through the fog that ran through his mind as well, finally recognizing its source. Grey Wolf had clouded their minds, knowing that she would attempt to sense their thoughts.

But all of her abilities had strengthened when she'd mated with Zander, including her gift for getting around mental obstacles. Light dawned an instant before Sebastian opened his mouth to speak.

"Let him talk, Zander."

Her mate nodded and took a step back as Sebastian circled the table towards them. She felt his confidence, his elation and excitement at finally taking center stage. She steeled herself, knowing he was coming for her.

He stopped a few feet away from her, glancing between her and Zander, self-preservation keeping him from taking those last few steps.

"Mediator." He sneered the word. "You expect us to believe that this pint-sized Unborn came across a being as powerful as a Shadow Wolf, and not only discovered vital information, but escaped and lived to tell about it? How naïve do you think we are?"

Lux, who'd been standing silently beside his parents, took a step forward, his voice raised as he addressed the Vampires who lined the walls. "Many of you were there when she arrived. You witnessed her collapse. It took all my knowledge to heal her from the wounds she had received, wounds kept from mending on their own by the work of the Shadow."

Nods of agreement were seen as the witnesses recalled the ragged state she had been in when she first entered Haven. Sebastian glared at the interruption.

"In spite of that *helpful* bit of information, we cannot be swayed so easily. My family fought with distinction in the war. No Abbadon rested until every last Shadow was wiped off the face of the earth. We left none alive. I think there may very well *be* a plot against the Truebloods..." He paused for effect as he glanced around at his rapt audience.

"But I think it is one of an Unborn making. And I believe Zander Sariel is in it up to his neck."

Lux held his father back as Zander calmly quieted the crowd, understanding why Regina had asked him to step back. Sebastian was about to do their job for them. He took a step closer to Regina, just in case, and his eyes returned once more to the doorway. Where was Kit?

Sebastian raised his hands and pointed at the shawl around Regina's neck, removing it with flamboyant drama. Zander clenched his fists as she paled and her hand fluttered defensively over the necklace. The garnets were immediately recognizable to every Elder at the table.

The shock in the room was palpable, exactly as Sebastian had anticipated. "I was stunned too, when I realized that our renowned Mediator, member of the purest, noblest bloodline in our history had been forced by our cursed genetics to mate with an Unborn. And not just any Unborn, but a member of the Deva Clan, Elizabeth's little band of terrorists."

Sebastian flung his white-blond hair over his shoulders, icy eyes glittering with a frenzied light. "It is against our laws, the very fabric of our society, to create or even associate with Unborns. Yet Zander Sariel has merged with one in Unity, mated with her, through no fault of his own. Most of you know how the mating fever can weaken even the most honorable of men."

He smirked and raised his eyebrow, drawing a few

uncomfortable chuckles from the crowd.

Zander glanced over at Lux and rolled his eyes, trying to calm his agitated brother before he did anything rash. Given enough time, Sebastian would reveal himself. He had always had more ego than intelligence.

"My soul knew you, my grathita. Were we not bound by genetics, I would still have taken you as my own."

He watched as his mate smiled in acknowledgment. She could not doubt his feelings, not when they were as clear to her as her own. It didn't stop the sting of Abbadon's attack...but it made it easier to bear.

"By your own judgments, at the very least, Zander should be banished, resign his position as Mediator for our community and join the ranks of the outcast along with his Unborn and her people. What a tragedy for a Vampire, trained his entire life for this position, to be brought so low. Another victim of our instinctual urge to mate."

He could tell the crowd wasn't sure what to think of that. Zander was a fair and well-liked Mediator, to banish him because of something as sacred and spiritual as a mate-bond made many of them hesitate.

"But he can be the *last* casualty. If this has shown us anything, it's that we can no longer survive as we have been. We are a dying race, a race whose blood is continuously tainted by necessity rather than choice. But Zander can be the last of our brethren, the last brother or sister, friend or relative to be doomed to such a horrific fate. I, Sebastian Abbadon, have found the key to our salvation!"

"What nonsense are you spouting, Younger Abbadon?" Elder Meroth stood, his chair thrown back in agitation. "Unity is *not* a horrific fate. It is a gift from the Mother Goddess. Without a mate of your own, it is impossible for you to understand."

Sebastian held up his hand in a conciliatory gesture, his pretense of respect obvious for all to see. "Elder, you mistake me. Those who have been blessed by the Mother to find their mates within our species, well they are gifted indeed. But aren't the Clan Trust Elders the ones who saw the need to outlaw Unborn creation and cohabitation?

"Aren't you the ones who have made the incredibly wise decision to keep us as separate from the Were communities as possible? I do not disagree with your wisdom, but it is certainly a challenge when over half of our species cannot find their mate among our numbers, or even among those humans who cross our path.

"Unity may be a gift, but didn't the Mother also give us the gift of invention, of discovery? And if I have used that to discover a serum guaranteed to alter any female Vampire into a fertile, breedable mate for *any* male—shouldn't that also be considered a gift from our Goddess?"

There was no stopping the disbelieving roar that came from the crowd. Several Elders attempted to bang on the table, but it took Zander stepping forward, hands elevated in a bid for silence, to finally end the cacophony.

"Until I *am* officially resigned and banished due to the laws that the Younger Abbadon so regretfully pointed out, I am still Mediator. This is a meeting of the Clan Trust and if calm cannot be maintained, then I will have no choice but to clear the room."

Sebastian's father stood, unable to contain his excitement as he looked at his peers. "I could hardly believe it myself, but it's true. My son has found a way to turn childless alliances into mated pairs, pairs capable of bearing young. There need be no more illicit matches, no more diluting of bloodlines. It's a miracle!"

"The Younger Abbadon has never struck me as a scientist." Zander looked to Elder Jazel, who had been silent until now, stroking his beard in thought as he spoke. "He has far too little patience for that. Sebastian, how did you come across this discovery of yours?"

"Who cares how he came across it? It's blasphemy." Elder Magriel pounded her small fist on the table before her.

"You know our origins as well as I. The Mother ensured the peace for all her children, gave us the blessing of Unity to balance our curse of darkness."

Zander moved to stand beside Regina, feeling through their connection the rage breaking over Sebastian at the Elder's words.

Sebastian spun towards Elder Magriel, planting both his hands on the table, caging her in, strands of hair falling into his blazing eyes as he leaned close.

"Cursed. You said it, Magriel, not I. It is a bedtime story for fools and children. Yet we obey. Has any one of you ever seen the Mother? *Any* of you ever been struck down for a trespass you violated? Why do we confine ourselves, limit ourselves? Why do we hide from humanity, when we should rule it? We could be gods to them, and yet we scurry around in shadows like rats. Because we needed them for mating—for survival? Well we can take what we need and more, and we no longer have to mate with those lesser beings. *I* have seen to that. I—"

"You, you, you. Your brother was right, that *is* all you can talk about."

Almost as one, the room looked towards the doorway at the newest arrivals. Zander smiled as he heard Regina gasp when she saw the unusual foursome.

Kit, Elizabeth, Nicolette and he would venture to guess that the young man in chains was Arygon Dydarren. He hadn't expected to see him here.

A few angered Vampires stepped forward, the two founders of the most infamous Unborn clan a prize too tempting to ignore. Kit slid his sword out of its sheath, stepping in front of the trio with an intimidating snarl.

"They come at my request, with information relevant to the initial reason I brought you all here. Let them pass." Zander worried that his words may have lost some of their power as the younger hoodlums hesitated before finally backing down.

Liz strode forward in all her cocky glory, red curls rioting down her back, leather vest and pants making her look more like a biker chick than the head of a clan.

Nicolette followed close behind, as elegant as she'd been described. They each held a chain that connected to a silver collar around the young pack leader's neck.

Arygon looked as if he'd been in one hell of a fight, but his expression showed only mild irritation.

Liz walked straight towards Regina, looking her over with maternal thoroughness before embracing her briskly. "What happened to your hair, Reggie? These inbred Truebloods turning you grey?"

Regina had a bemused smile on her face, and Zander felt her confusion at the presence of her sire, but also an unmistakable swell of relief. She looked at him in question.

"Lux sent a message to Liz prior to the fire. They've been friends a long time, and he didn't want her to worry.

She was already on her way when I realized that she might be able to help us. It seems she had the same thought and brought the necessary reinforcements. At the very least she can take you out of here should things get too...sticky."

He knew Regina was worried about her sire, but she hadn't

known Elizabeth when Malcolm had been alive. Elizabeth hadn't been afraid of anything, even then. And it was Malcolm Abbadon himself, the finest warrior of his generation, who'd trained her in the art of combat.

The vein in Sebastian's temple had started to pulse, his eyelid twitching as he looked at the embodiment of his family's ruination.

Zander knew he had always blamed her for Malcolm turning his back on his good name and awe-inspiring war career. His own brother, whose reputation he had rode so long on the coattails of, choosing to create an Unborn, marrying her in a human ceremony when they realized they could not mate.

Sebastian had wanted her too, not enough to honor her, but enough to attempt to plant the seeds of doubt in each of their minds.

Had Lux not discovered his machinations and informed the couple, he might have succeeded. He had even sought her out when Malcolm had been murdered, imagining he could have his brother's leavings. That was one of the reasons she'd needed to disappear. It was no secret that most of Sebastian's playthings did not last long.

His lust had gone hand-in-hand with his loathing, since he and his father had led the initial battle cry for complete separation, to make the creations of Unborn illegal instead of merely taboo. Using Malcolm's memory, they finally succeeded.

"Little Lizzy, what a pleasant surprise. And you brought a pet. Is he one of the Weres that murdered your husband for you?"

Regina and Nicolette placed restraining hands on Liz's shoulders, both glaring daggers at Sebastian. Zander knew it was time to bring this free-for-all to an end.

"Elders hear me. We came in perfect trust, but one among

us did not honor that oath. One among us has betrayed, and has been betrayed in turn. I would ask you to hear Regina, formerly of the Clan Deva, now a Sariel and *my mate*, tell you what she knows. We sought to hide nothing from you, as the Sariel necklace can testify. I called this meeting for the good of all my people, of all the species, and I ask your indulgence."

The Elders nodded, returning slowly to their seats. Elder Abbadon, huffing in protest, last of all. Zander drew Regina to the front of the table, sending her all his love and support as she shared what she knew.

She reiterated what she'd told them upon her arrival at Haven, that she had been captured by Grey Wolf of the Shadow while spying on Dydarren's Pack.

He noticed the two Devas cringing in horror as she spoke of her torture at Grey's hands. He had humiliated her, starved her and branded her with his dark magick as he shared his plans for the future.

"He said *he'd* found a potion to reverse the curse of the Goddess. He'd discovered a way to mate and breed with the woman of his choice. It was the key to the renewing of his people. And the end of all Truebloods."

"Lies! Lies!" Sebastian turned as if to attack Regina where she stood, but before he could move Kit was in front of him.

Though the Sariel guards rarely showed themselves, no one could mistake that they had seen one. And you would have to be a fool to face one down alone. Sebastian was no fool.

"She speaks the truth." Arygon Dydarren's rough voice bounced off the high ceilings of the room. Zander caught the eye of each Elder, before nodding to Arygon, signaling him to continue.

"I was with Grey Wolf when he took her. I had no idea of his plans. I believed he had come to help my pack settle a dispute." Liz snorted, but Arygon just clenched his jaw and continued.

"He tricked me. He brainwashed my Beta and most of the males of my pack, teaching them the dark ways, luring them with promises of power and blood.

When I realized what he had planned, I attempted to stop him. I brought down two of my own who were guarding the cave where Regina was being held...gave her a chance to escape."

Zander felt Regina's shock, but when she searched Arygon's mind, she realized it was true. She hadn't questioned their absence, had only taken advantage of it, crawling out of her prison. He supposed he owed the Were for that.

"I heard his plans, heard him say he would make her his mate. He laughed about the Trueblood he had under his thumb, the one he had tricked into doing his dirty work for him." Arygon stared pointedly at Sebastian, meeting his rage-filled expression with arrogant pride.

"The serum he gave you will fail. It will render every female who takes it incapable of reproducing, even if she were to find her mate. It will end your species forever, while the Shadow Wolves steadily grow in strength and number, as numerous as humanity, but a thousand times more deadly."

Zander noted the disgusted looks on the faces of the Elders as they studied the Younger Abbadon and his father.

Sebastian's expression turned hunted. He grabbed his head in pain before turning to run from the room, his movement too swift and surprising for anyone to follow.

His actions made his guilt clear to all. His "discovery" had almost ended the race of Vampires for good. The Elder Abbadon stood as if to follow, but was subdued in an instant by a handful of younger men from the Meroth Clan, who, following a nod from their Elder, led him away.

"Sari? Sari? Where is she? She was just here a moment ago. Get your hands off me. I am an *Elder.*" Several of the Abbadon Clan shuffled guiltily, but none made a single move to help their leader. Many knelt, lowering their heads and spreading their hands, palms up, showing their desire to transfer loyalties. They had all been fooled.

Zander felt a hand on his shoulder and turned to find Lux, his face tight with worry. "Glynn Magriel is not here as she said she would be. Sebastian might have had something to do with that. He would have believed she was the only threat to his plans."

"I agree. I'll send Kit and Max to find her. Right now we need to get our family and friends to safety. I have a feeling this battle is far from over."

Lux nodded, hurrying to his parents' side as Zander took his place at the head of the table. Meroth stood and walked towards him, turning to address his fellow Elders when he reached Zander's side.

"Once again a Sariel Mediator has shown loyalty, even when he knew his reward could be banishment or worse, due to our mating laws. The Younger Abbadon was right about one thing. If we don't change as a people, we will die. If we continue as we have been, xenophobic and isolated, there will be no new generations, there will be no more Vampires. Let us think on this tonight, until we are called together again when Sebastian and his father are tried for treason."

"And what of the current law? A Sariel, the truest bloodline in the history of our race is mated to an Unborn. What do we do about that?" Elder Jazel had no taint of disrespect in his voice, merely curiosity.

"The Mother Goddess brought them together for a reason, Elder Jazel. Sariel's mate has already risked great peril to herself to warn us all. A risk she was not obligated to take. I believe this is a law that has shown no benefit to our people, and has only caused hardship and pain."

Elder Magriel stood with quiet dignity, allowing her daughter, who'd been hovering nearby, to lead her away.

The crowd quickly dispersed, most overcome by the startling revelations the night had revealed. Zander's parents, at the urging of Lux, accepted Meroth's generous offer to stay with him while their sons joined the search for Sebastian and the Shadow Wolf.

Zander looked to find Regina and her two fellow Devas deep in conversation, the joy on her face lightening his heart.

Arygon stood behind them, unable to go far due to the collar around his neck. His arms were crossed in apparent aggravation, but his gaze was fixed on Lux as he stood laughing with his mother across the room. As much as the Were tried, there was no hiding the lust in his eyes.

Regina caught Zander's eye and smiled at his thoughts. He jerked his head towards the door, indicating their need for haste. It didn't take long before their mismatched band was headed past the gates of Abbadon Keep.

Though he knew there were dangers ahead, Zander couldn't help but feel Regina's thrill of relief. They had done it. Sebastian had made it all too easy, but there had still been several close calls.

Everyone had been so shocked at Abbadon's betrayal that they hadn't stopped to wonder why a Shadow Wolf had wanted to mate with Regina, as Arygon had testified.

He felt no guilt at not volunteering the information about her gifts to the Elders in front of the volatile audience.

Tempers had run high, too much had been learned. But they had accepted the pairing, which meant the rest of the

Trueblood community would have no choice but to accept her as well.

It meant nothing to him. He would have left his home and family behind in an instant if any of them had refused to accept his *grathita*. But Regina cared. And because she was relieved, he was as well.

The Sariel Guard appeared as if forming from the mist, and he picked up his pace. He couldn't stop the feeling of foreboding that shivered through his veins. He wouldn't rest until Regina was secure in his family's underground fortress once more.

Chapter Ten

"So you and Zander, huh? I *never* would've seen that coming." Reggie looked at her sire from beneath her lashes, her gaze wary. Knowing Liz as she did, it was still impossible to predict her reaction to the news.

"Are you upset?"

Liz slid her arm through Reggie's as they walked through the night, her head tilted as if in thought, red hair gleaming in each stray shaft of moonlight. "About what? The fact that you figured out how to block me when I tried to find you? Well, I *was* a bit upset about that. We've been frantic these last few weeks, especially after that story little Maria told us. She was so panicked her father begged us to make her forget the entire experience.

When she told us you had been taken, and I couldn't reach you through our mental connection...I thought you might be dead. We went to the last place she'd seen you. That's where we found him." She jerked her head towards Arygon, who'd been stomping in silent exasperation behind them.

As Reggie's attention fell on their handsome pest, he wrapped one fist around the chains connected to his collar and shook them tellingly. "Before we go any further do you think we can get me out of this contraption? We've lost site of the Keep, and it itches."

Nicolette appeared beside him, her graceful fingers working the hidden lock as she smiled up at the grumpy-looking Were. "It's a shame. This is such a good look for you." Reggie's eyes widened as Nicolette responded to his low growl with a lighthearted laugh. Something had definitely changed between the Devas and Dydarren since she'd been gone.

"He was close to death when we found him. Thankfully, the Shadow had been so distraught by your disappearance he left Arygon to face his own brainwashed pack. We wouldn't have been able to save him if Grey Wolf had had his way with him."

Reggie watched as Arygon flung the hated silver to the snow, stretching his neck and rolling his shoulders in relief. She saw the still-healing wound that the collar had hidden—a jagged pink scar that ran the length of his jugular.

The fact that he'd survived at all was amazing. And that he'd been shamed and attacked by his own men because he'd helped her to get away, hadn't been lost on her.

She turned and walked towards him, reaching up to kiss his cheek. His green eyes widened, his cheekbones flushing as he looked at her. "Thank you."

He shrugged her words away, but his lips quirked slightly, as if fighting a smile.

Nicolette came up on Reggie's other side, guiding her, along with Liz, back into the group still heading back towards the castle ruins.

She didn't look at Reggie, but it was easy to feel the remorse and sadness that surrounded her. "I'll never forgive myself for sending you into danger alone. I was so worried about Hannah, so angry, that I didn't think of every possibility."

Reggie tried to interrupt but Nicolette continued undaunted. "Now I realize that this entire situation is my fault. It was my thoughtless actions all those years ago that started our skirmishes with the Dydarren Pack. And my pride that refused to end the animosity. There is no way to make amends for the havoc I have wrought."

Arygon surprised them all by sliding his arm around Nicolette's slender shoulders and squeezing lightly. "I am just as much to blame. I let my pain and anger rule me, let my losses cloud my judgment. I was a fool. A fool that willingly sold his soul to the devil. If you can forgive me, take your enemy into your home and heal him—then I can do no less. Let it be done between us."

Reggie's eyes widened as she watched the always-controlled Madame wipe tears from her eyes, nodding her agreement. Though her curiosity was killing her, she refused to invade this obviously private moment by satisfying it with a little mental snooping.

"Back to the subject at hand." Liz drew Reggie's attention once more, her dimples peeking out as she smirked humorously.

"I have to admit I was surprised when Lux told me you had found your way to Haven. And more than shocked to be informed that you were his brother's *grathita*." She looked over her shoulder at the Sariel brothers, who'd been deep in quiet conversation behind them.

"Before my husband died, he would often say that he was Abbadon by birth, but it was the Sariels that he considered his family. As honorable as Malcolm was, that is high praise indeed."

Liz sighed. "I sometimes wonder if he would agree with a lot of the choices I've made. He believed that the future of his people depended on new blood, the merging and cooperation with other species, humans and Were. He said that was what his goddess had in mind all along. I just thought she could use a little nudge."

She shrugged and began walking a little faster, as if she could outrun her own thoughts. "I'll never know the answer, but I do know he would heartily approve of the match between you and Zander. And if you had to go and get yourself mixed up with the Truebloods, I suppose I can only be grateful that you had the intelligence to hitch your wagon to the likes of Sariel. He's a good man."

This night was one shocking revelation after another. Reggie would never have imagined that Elizabeth would condone her mating, or that she would express doubt about her own actions when she never had before. And Nicolette and Arygon walking together as allies? It was inconceivable. If she wasn't witnessing it with her own eyes she'd never believe it.

They'd just reached the rise of the last hill, the clear night making the crumbling walls of the old castle visible, when she froze. It felt as if a heavy cloud of blackness surrounded her, suffocating her with terror and remembered pain. She knew this feeling.

"Regina? Regina, run!"

She never got the chance. In the space of a breath they were surrounded. Seven Sariel guards and their six charges looked out into the crowd of angry Weres, all fully transformed and closing in with obvious purpose. There had to be at least one hundred of the fur-covered beasts.

"Transform, Regina. Fly away. Now!"

Reggie noticed Zander step closer to her, his body tensed and ready for battle, his fangs extended as he stared down their growling captors.

"I will not leave you."

"Damn it, do as you're told!"

"Little Gypsy. You have led me on a merry chase, haven't you?"

The crowd of beasts parted, allowing Grey Wolf to sweep past them and enter into the circle they'd made around Reggie and the others. The guards snarled, the clanking of metal indicating that they'd raised their swords, but Zander motioned to them for stillness. This was a Shadow Wolf. And it was too close to Regina for his piece of mind.

There was a rustling behind him, and Reggie saw the distinctive white-blond heads of Sebastian Abbadon and his sister Sari appear on either side of the smiling Grey.

"I trust introductions aren't in order?" Grey's grin widened as he took in the grim faces of his audience.

"The twins here have more than made up for their brother's senseless slaughtering of my brethren. They might be lacking in loyalty, but they more than make up for it with their thirst for power. A trait I can only admire."

He walked over to Lux, with a nod at Sari. She took Reggie by surprise, spinning her around to hold a small, sharp blade to her throat.

"Just a little insurance," he murmured to Zander as he passed, stopping in front of Lux and looking him over, the twinkling blackness of his gaze proof he was enjoying his moment.

"I suppose you're all wondering how we found the entrance to your little hideaway? Everyone knew you had one, but no one had the slightest idea as to its location. Until recently, of course." He raised his arm and one of the nearby Weres tossed a limp body onto the ground at Lux's feet.

Reggie gasped as she realized who it was. Joel. He lay there, eyes wide and lifeless, a hole in his chest where his heart used to be.

"*Bastard.*" Lux made a move as if to strike Grey down, but Arygon grabbed him, holding him back.

Grey laughed loudly, throwing back his head. "Don't look so upset, boy. You may have lost one lover, but it looks as though you've another all primed to take his place."

"Let them go." Grey turned sharply at the sound of Reggie's voice, which echoed in his head as she used her abilities to tempt him. He strode over to her, his black cloak rippling in the breeze as he grasped her chin tightly in his hand.

"What makes you think you have any sway with me, Gypsy? The news of your connubial bliss has spread, my dear, and your only hold over me was the promise of your gifts. Gifts you now share with that spineless bloodsucker."

He pressed her lower lip down with his thumb, staring at it as if fascinated, so close she could feel his darkness like stinging needles on her skin.

"Luckily that, like every other problem I've encountered, is easily remedied. But first things first. Sari?"

"Yes, my love?"

"Kill your brother."

"Yes, my love."

Grey turned Reggie just in time for her to see Sari dive for a horrified Sebastian, stabbing him in the heart. She was smiling serenely as if she'd done nothing wrong while he dropped to the ground beside her.

"Do you see what she's willing to do for me? She appreciates my unique...charms." He looked at Liz's pale face and grumbled impatiently.

"I did you all a favor. *He* is the one who actually killed Malcolm, I merely helped him make it look like a random Were attack. He became the heir to his father's clan, and I got my foot in the door of your vaunted Clan Trust. I even forced poor Sari to cozy up to the young Mediator here. Not a very satisfying job, to hear her tell it."

Reggie felt the shock that reverberated through her small party. Grey Wolf had been planning this for *that* long? He and Sebastian had killed Malcolm? That was over tow hundred and fifty years ago. The idea didn't do anything to calm her nerves.

Grey brandished a small, empty vial, waving it with a flourish as he bent over Sebastian's frozen form. Gathering the heart's blood into the tiny container, he stood and looked into the adoring doe eyes of the last surviving Abbadon sibling.

"Sari, my dearest, I have one more thing I need from you." Sari looked up at him and Reggie felt a chill of dread thread up her spine.

Zander caught the vibe and stepped forward, only to be halted when the Werewolves nearest Reggie stepped on either side, a clear warning that held him immobile.

"You see, there is only one way for me to have what I truly desire. It is exceedingly difficult to separate a mated pair, the requirements for that kind of magick nearly impossible to come by. You, sweet Sari, you and Sebastian are the only ones who can help me."

In an instant, Grey had slipped the blade from her lax fingers. It was still dripping with the blood of her twin when he stabbed it into her heart.

With a twist he pulled it from her, dropping her without compunction after he had gathered some of her blood into his vial as well.

"Betrayal of the blood." He murmured as he capped the vial and slid it back into his cloak. "What could be worse than the betrayal of family? Sebastian killed his brother; sweet Sari killed her own twin. I honestly couldn't have planned it better."

176

Reggie knew then that he had no intention of letting a little thing like her mate-bond with Zander get in the way of his plans for her. She also realized that the very thing she feared, her presence putting the people she loved in danger, was really happening. She had one chance to save them.

"Regina—wait!"

But it was too late. She was soaring, flying through the night as fast as her wings would allow. In the form of a raven she flew away from the shocked Weres, away from her sire and her mate, knowing with every fiber of her being that the obsessive Shadow Wolf would be compelled to follow...but just in case, she sent him a taunt.

"You want me, Grey? Come and get me."

Zander watched his mate turn to a speck in the sky, part of him relieved, part horrified that he would no longer be able to protect her. He heard her taunt as well, knew the Shadow wouldn't be able to resist. Before he could reach Grey, the sorcerer took off after Regina, several Werewolves close behind.

"Kill them! All but the Mediator! Hold him until I return." Zander heard the shout moments before all Hell broke loose.

He joined Arygon and Lux around the two women as the crowd of snarling Weres charged towards them.

"Oh, Nic, look, aren't they sweet?" Liz laughed an instant before a large panther leapt over Zander's shoulder, taking the nearest Were down, her fangs ripping through its throat with ease.

"Lux, we need a little light on the subject!" Zander was morphing as the words left his mouth, the large golden bear quickly diving into the fray.

He could see Lux, surrounded by Arygon and Nicolette,

closing his eyes and raising his arms to the sky, calling on the elements.

One of Grey's minions jumped on the bear's back, attempting to pin him down. He flipped the mongrel over his shoulder, one giant swipe of his paw slashing open the Were's chest.

He heard a battle cry and looked up in time to see Kit and the other guards stride into the thick of the battle.

They expanded before his eyes, not morphing as he had done, just—growing. Already hulking brutes, their expansion set them head and shoulders above even the sizable Werewolves. They were a terrifying and more-than-welcome sight as they swung their swords with controlled violence, cleaving their way easily through the crowd.

Zander felt pain burn through his side as a set of curving claws caught him by surprise. Turning with a growl, he rolled, pulling his attacker to the ground.

In moments their struggle was over, as he ripped out the heart of his combatant. They fell so easily, these Weres. The Shadow had obviously neglected to teach them the darker arts, and in their frenzied, hypnotic state, they seemed to have no control over their natural abilities. They fought like mindless, feral dogs.

Lightning struck, charging the air with the scent of ozone, followed by the distinct aroma of charred fur. Lux had called the storm.

Several Werewolves converged, heading towards Zander's brother, determined to stop him. Nicolette had gone to aid Liz, and the guards were still surrounded by a never-ending swarm of Weres, leaving no one to protect Lux. Except Arygon.

Zander watched as the pack leader, standing out against his attackers with his startling silver fur, took all comers. He knew many were from his own den, but Arygon showed no hesitation as he struck them down while Lux focused on directing the bolts of energy.

The bear that was Zander turned, large paw extended for a powerful swipe, only to slice through empty air. The Shadow Wolf's remaining followers were scattering, running away to lick their wounds.

He shifted back, walking over to where the others had gathered, a little bloody and battle-weary, but otherwise unharmed. There was, however, no time for celebration.

"Liz, you and I need to work together to find Regina. Lux, we need any warrior the Meroth and Jazal clans can spare. Grey Wolf must be found. The Trust should also be informed that Sebastian and Sari Abbadon have been murdered." The small, serious gathering agreed in silence.

Zander walked up to Arygon, who'd bent to scoop up some snow, placing it on the back of his neck.

The Were looked up with narrowed eyes as Zander placed a hand on his shoulder, kneeling beside him on the wet, frozen ground. "You have saved the life of my mate and protected my brother from harm. You have my loyalty, and the fealty and protection of my House, for as long as you desire."

Arygon's expression was one of humbled surprise as he nodded slowly. He looked up at Lux, who silently held out his hand to lift the subdued Arygon to a standing position once more.

Zander stood and turned in the direction he'd seen his raven fly, Liz and three of the Sariel guards following in his wake. He used his connection to reach out to Regina, his only solace that the fragile thread between them hadn't been severed.

"Grathita. *My* priya, *where are you?*"

Regina was in the dark, walking swiftly through a familiar wood. It was the one she had seen in her dream when she'd been trapped in Unity sleep. Images flashed in her mind—her Daj Mia, the Mother Goddess, Zander. It was still too jumbled to make out, but she knew it was important.

"Reader..."

She turned, looking carefully around the gnarled trunks and bare, jagged branches for the whispered voice. There, between two bent and ancient trees, stood a small, older woman in deep purple robes. She could have been a clone of Elder Magriel, but for the spiral tattooing that started at her forehead and covered her face, disappearing down her neck into the robe's folds.

"Priestess Magriel."

"Please, child, call me Glynn. Come closer, Regina, our time is short."

Reggie walked forward, noticing two younger Vampires, male and female, both dressed in white robes, standing on either side of the Healer.

When she stood in front of Glynn Magriel she felt a wash of love and peace, and the power of it was so profound that she suddenly felt like weeping. She was led to a fallen trunk, smooth with age, and Glynn sat beside her.

"Your gift has brought you so much. Sorrow, knowledge, isolation. And love. Yet you still have no true understanding of what it means to be what you are. And what it could mean to our people."

Reggie knew she must have looked as confused as she felt when Glynn nodded. "You've heard the myth. You know that because of arrogance, the Mother gave certain gifts to faithful group of women, gave them the knowledge to save humanity and destroy the monsters that threatened their existence." She motioned to herself with a self-effacing shrug.

"Those women were called Readers, because of their ability to hear and understand the innermost thoughts of everyone around them. Able to see a lie, to be forewarned of danger. They were a sisterhood, known to all by the very distinctive mark on their forehead. A circle of black, symbolizing sight through the darkness and secret knowledge."

Reggie brushed the mark on her forehead with her fingers. The mark her Daj Mia had given to her on her sixteenth birthday. The mark she was told had been worn by every female member of her maternal line for as far back as any could recall. Her heart was pounding as she realized what Glynn was implying.

"When the bloody wars for supremacy spilled into human villages and homes, when the carnage threatened to wipe out all of her children, the Mother wove into them a knowledge that most would be unable to bear. The antithesis of creation. A tool of destruction too powerful for most to control.

That 'gift' was given to the Readers, and they used it to destroy the most powerful minds of that generation, *Were* and *Vampire*. Some of the Readers went insane themselves, unable to carry the weight of the gift, unable to face what they could do. What they had done. But we know now that at least one survived, and kept the faith of the Mother all this time, buried within her family line."

Glynn smiled sympathetically and Reggie realized she was shaking her head in denial. The Healer was mistaken, wasn't she? Yet again she momentarily wished for the ignorance of her youth, before she knew that Vampires were real, before she became part of their most hallowed myths.

"It's true, Regina. Your grandmother would have shared

what she knew if you hadn't been taken away from her so early. And if my people, *our* people, hadn't been so afraid of the past, they would have heeded the words of the Healers ages ago, those who study the mind and follow the intuitive path, the peaceful path of the Goddess. Instead they forbade any member of our species to create an Unborn Reader, to mate with a Reader, on punishment of immediate death for both."

Reggie gasped, standing and taking a few halting steps before turning to face the priestess. "So by Trueblood law, Zander could be killed for mating with me? Does he know that? And Liz. Liz could be killed for having created me in the first place?"

Glynn nodded. "Yes, dear, and of course Zander knew. He is the Mediator. He was spoon-fed Trueblood law since he was born. But you are his true mate, his destiny. Love is an amazing power, the one element none of us have ever been able to control, not with all our gifts."

She laughed and shook her head. "As for Elizabeth, I wouldn't be too sure she didn't know exactly what you were when she decided to bring you over. Malcolm was a faithful worshipper of the Goddess. He and I would often discuss the possibility of the Readers still existing in the world. He believed in the Message of the Goddess."

"The Message of the Goddess? What Message?"

"Yes, Healer...tell her the message. Tell her of the last words spoken to the leaders of the Werewolf and Vampire races before the Goddess ran back to her little moon, never to be seen again."

She hadn't felt him. She'd been too distracted by the information Glynn was sharing to keep her guard up. Too late she saw the initiates of the Healer drop bloody to the ground, several large Weres quickly taking their place around Glynn

Magriel.

Reggie felt his hand on her shoulder, shivering once again at the darkness he exuded as he turned her around.

"She seems to be at a loss for words. Allow me. Our matriarchs had the same story after all, the same message. Just as the moon renews itself again and again, the goddess said we would have a chance at redemption. Only together could we fill our world with light. The key lies with you, sweet Gypsy. A Reader from a true line. A Reader who will find her mate with Vampire or Were. She will share her powers with him and their children will shape the future of our world, bringing a new day to our civilization."

Grey smiled, his eyes alight with a crazed intensity as he studied her. "I knew from the moment I saw you, that all the plans I had been working towards were merely preparation for this. For you. My destiny. I will gather my scattered brethren, and we will create our armies anew. And this time, we will win the day. And I will rule. With you by my side, as the Mother intended."

His grip on her tightened, and he began to pull her away from the tiny clearing. Glynn grasped her hand tightly, taking her by surprise. She hadn't even seen the woman move.

"You can stop him, Regina. The gift the Mother gave, you have it. It's a dark place, terrifying. The absence of light can drive some insane. But you can control it. You can use it. You were born to do it. Look within. Do not be afraid."

It was only a moment in time. Glynn's hand was ripped away by one of Grey Wolf's henchmen. It seemed as if everything was moving in slow motion, the yellowed claws stained with drying blood as the Were raised his muscled arm to strike the Healer down.

Something clicked inside her. The images from her dream

became clear.

She looked at the threatening Were, deep into his mind and attacked. The arm that had been in mid-swing dropped, all motor control gone as the Werewolf fell to his knees with a chilling scream.

Grey had gone pale at the scene before him. As Reggie faced him she could see herself in his eyes, knew that her own had gone from gold to black, pupils expanding as she reached into the darkness of his soul.

She saw it all, all of his twisted plans, his sadism. And past that, she saw the horrific training he was forced into, a child, a pup made to see death, love death.

There was only one corner of his heart that hadn't been tainted by the need for vengeance, the hatred of humanity and Vampires. In that corner she saw a young girl. Sylvain. His sister.

Without mercy she pushed past that, finding the core of him hidden away, cloaked in shadows. She tore through his protection with ease, forced him to face the horror of what he was.

And with a thought she unmade his mind.

As if standing outside herself, she watched this screaming mass that used to be a powerful Shadow Wolf.

She felt no surprise when she noted the arrival of Zander and Elizabeth. The guards, still in their terrifyingly gargantuan forms, quickly dispatched the remaining Weres.

She watched as Zander turned Grey towards him, his fingernails elongated and sharpened, punching through his chest, ending his life. Before Reggie could.

"Pull it back, Regina. I'm here, my love. It's alright, I'm here."

Liz walked up to Grey Wolf's body, unable to find an outlet

for her rage, and spit on his corpse. Reggie knew Grey had put the idea of murder into Sebastian's weak-willed mind, and she knew Liz was wishing she'd had the chance to kill him herself.

She couldn't move, couldn't blink. She wondered if she would ever be able to come back from this darkness, to feel warmth again. She felt the Healer's touch like a balm on her stinging flesh.

"You did it, Reader. Everyone you love is safe. Rest now."

And she did.

Chapter Eleven

"You know you want to. Its all you've been able to think about."

Reggie smiled over her shoulder at her mate from her position by the tinted window. "Not *all* I've been able to think about."

Zander leered comically and waggled his eyebrows from his position on the bed. "Well, I was trying to be a gentleman. Who knew the goddess would mate me to such a tireless sex fiend?"

She gasped in outrage and looked for something to throw, but he grabbed her before she got the chance, rolling her beneath him on the bed.

The cottage he'd bought for them was right on the North Sea, and Regina could hear the rushing sound of the ocean as she looked into her lover's sapphire eyes. She never imagined such happiness existed.

Thanks to the Healer and her students, Reggie had come out of her experience with nothing more than the occasional nightmare and a few more strands of grey in her hair. Zander thought they were sexy, so she'd decided to leave them as they were.

Liz and Nicolette had gone back to their home on Lago Maggiore, but only after she'd promised to visit soon. She was family, after all. And things would be different now.

The members of the Dydarren Pack were under new leadership, Arygon having stepped down and deciding to remain in England for a while. His cousin Ty, though no natural Alpha, had agreed to end the conflict and to serve as Beta for the Dydarrens while Arygon was away.

"When do we have to go back?" She tried to hide the wistfulness in her tone but she knew it was impossible. He always knew.

"Well, restructuring of The Trust needs to happen as soon as possible. But I see no reason why we can't hold it off, at least one more week."

His short sandy hair fell forward as he bent to kiss her brow. "Even the Mediator deserves to enjoy his honeymoon in peace. Besides, they aren't quite done rebuilding Haven."

Reggie knew they had to return soon, and not just for political reasons. The regretful eyes of her mate told her she was not alone in her worry for the younger Sariel.

Since the night Joel had been killed, Lux seemed to have withdrawn into himself. Reggie knew he felt guilty for not being there to protect his lover, for allowing him to leave without taking precautions. But that was just because of her abilities.

No one would know to look at Lux that he felt anything at all. Unless Arygon was around. The moment the cocky Werewolf showed up, which was surprisingly often of late, Lux couldn't hide his irritation.

Arygon didn't seem to mind. If anything it merely made him more determined to be underfoot, being exactly what she'd always called him. A pest.

She had a feeling about those two. And if she'd learned anything from Glynn, it was to pay attention to her intuitions. So it wasn't long after she'd left the Healers that Reggie had sought out Lux and Arygon.

She knew what it was like to be alone in the world, and she couldn't live with herself if she didn't attempt to find the young female Were whose face she'd seen in Grey Wolf's mind. Sylvain. She'd sent the unlikely duo to find her and bring her back. It had seemed...right somehow, she didn't question why.

Sliding her fingers up her mate's bulging arms, Reggie couldn't help but recall how he'd woken her this afternoon.

Pulled from sleep by the sound of her own screams as she came, Zander's hard cock thrusting deep as he curled around her from behind. It was better than any alarm clock. It was how she wanted to wake for the next thousand years.

"And so you shall."

Zander smiled and raised himself off the bed, pulling her along behind him. "No distracting your mate with feminine wiles. It's time to get ready."

Reggie pulled against his grip, to no avail. "Are you sure?"

"Grathita, would I ever put you in danger?"

She sighed, her shoulders relaxing as she wrapped her arms around him and smiled. "Never."

He nodded in arrogant satisfaction at her reply, before slathering her face and arms with thick, white cream. He looked at the directions on the bottle, then added a bit more to her nose, before spreading the cream over his visible flesh as well.

He put the cap back on the bottle with a snap, taking her hand and heading for the back door that would lead them to the beach.

It was close to sunset. After two hundred years, she could barely remember what that looked like. But she was about to see it again, after all this time.

Zander had told her that when they'd joined in Unity, she'd gotten more than the ability to shift and bear his children.

She'd also gotten the strength of his age and bloodline—his ability to be out in the sun. Only at sunrise and sunset, but for Reggie, it was more than enough. It was a miracle.

His hand touched the knob and she covered it with her own. "*I love you.*"

"*And I love you, Regina mine. Now come, I want to see for myself how your eyes rival the gold of the day, how your skin glows. I want to see you dance for me at sunset.*"

She smiled, nodding as they opened the door together. The air was still cool with the bite of winter, but it didn't bother her. She felt the unfamiliar warmth heat her face an instant before she saw it. So bright she had to close her eyes until, ever prepared, Zander slid a pair of specialized sunglasses on her nose.

It was stunning. A myriad of glimmering colors swirled across the skyline, framing the fiery ball of the sun as it sunk slowly into the horizon. Tears filled her eyes at the beauty of it.

"*It cannot compare to you, my* priya.*"

She felt his hand in her own as they walked down the wooden steps that led to the beach. They stood together, ignoring the slight discomfort that prickled their skin at the weakening rays, and watched in silence until that final flash of light melted into the sea.

She turned to Zander, wiping the wetness from her cheeks with a watery chuckle. Who could have guessed when she went looking for sanctuary that she would find this—find him? That when she next walked into the sun, it would be the beginning of her life...and not the end.

These last few weeks her world had been turned completely upside down. She'd discovered that far from being an unimportant member of her clan, she was meant to be that first step in linking the species together once more. Were, Vampire and human.

And far from being alone in the world, kept at a distance because of her abilities, as she had been all her human life, she had a family. A mate. Someone whose love she never had to question. Thank the Mother.

As darkness fell and the stars began their shimmering dance in the sky, she looked up at her sexy blood-mate and grinned. His eyes went dark. She could feel his desire as he pulled her closer, and she knew he'd gotten her silent message.

Throwing her over his shoulder as she laughed, he strode with a speed no human could match back up the rickety steps to their cottage. Before they reached the door, Reggie realized they were both completely naked.

"I really want to know how you do that."

"I'll tell you anything, grathita. *But first...you owe me a dance."*

About the Author

Stolen away by a free-spirited Gypsy as a child (though she still swears she's my mother), I spent my childhood roaming the countryside, meeting fascinating characters and having amazing adventures. As the perpetual "new kid", my friends more often than not were found between the pages of a book...and in my own imagination. I read everything I could get my hands on. At the age of 11, I read my first romance and I've been hooked ever since.

I've been a nurse, a lead vocalist in several bands, a published lyricist and even a returning university student majoring in Anthropology and Mythology. Throughout all of my varied careers, I would sigh as I read one fantasy-filled story after another saying, "Someday I want to write one of those", until one day my husband said, "So do it". And I did. Now I can't imagine doing anything else.

To learn more about R.G. Alexander please visit www.rgalexander.com. Send an email to R.G. Alexander at r.g.alexander@hotmail.com.

One duel. Easy money. Then Gil fell for his opponent.

Crossing Swords
© 2008 Kirsten Saell

A straight duel to the death. A professional opponent who's paying him to win. This was going to be the easiest money Gil had ever earned. Except he never counted on his opponent being a woman. And he never counted on falling for her.

After avenging the brutal murder of her lover, all Lianon wants is to die a clean death. Too bad the man she hired doesn't do women, and he's furious over her deception. Not only does he renege on their contract, he has the gall to lock her up in his apartment—naked, no less!—to punish her for her ruse.

If she could just get her mind out of the gutter, she'd cut him a new smile. But ever since he saw through her boy's clothes, all she can think about is getting him naked, too.

But just when she's found something to live for, the father of her lover's murderer surfaces. He wants Lianon to die screaming—and he's all too happy to take Gil down with her.

Available now in ebook and print from Samhain Publishing.

Bullets won't bring down this killer. It'll take a vampire.

Trust the Night
© *2008 Sara Saint John*

Having survived a violent husband, homicide detective Beth Andrews has no patience for abusers. In her eyes, "Mad Jack" is committing the ultimate abuse against the women of Oklahoma City—murder—and she'll stop at nothing to bring him to justice. Even risk her own life.

The sexy "mind scientist" she's been paired with is a distraction she doesn't need, but he's getting under her skin in more ways than one. She spends her days investigating the murders. Nights, discovering Sam.

Criminal psychologist Sam Jordan knows he is two things Beth doesn't trust: a shrink, and a man. But Beth needs his help more than she knows, because like the killer they hunt, Sam is a vampire. And he's been pursuing Jack the Ripper for longer than Beth's been alive.

Revealing himself would do more than destroy her fragile trust. It could make her Mad Jack's next target.

Available now in ebook and print from Samhain Publishing.

Enjoy the following excerpt from Trust the Night...

Stakeouts were to be kept confidential, but something inside Beth superceded the requirement for secrecy. She needed to reveal this one to Sam—and with the telling, give him the right to know. Besides, it might be her last chance to hear his voice before tonight. Definitely a sound she wanted to take with her. She picked up the phone and dialed his number.

"Hello?" It was the old lady again.

"It's Detective Andrews. Is Sam still sleeping?"

"He won't mind waking for *you*, dear. Hold on, I'll get him."

Beth waited, wondering what Sam had told the woman. Who was she anyway? His housekeeper? His mother?

"Beth? Is anything wrong?"

The sound of his voice calmed her nerves. "Thank heavens," she said. "I didn't know if I'd get the chance to talk to you."

"Why? What's up?"

"I'm going undercover. Tonight we're setting a trap for the Ripper."

"No. You don't know what you're up against."

"Yes, Sam, I do. You did a very complete profile on him. Don't worry, I'll be surrounded by Oklahoma City's finest."

Exasperation filled his voice. "*You* don't understand. He's deadly. Far deadlier than you can imagine."

"Sam, I've seen what he does to his victims. Seen the blood smeared on his face. He's crazy. I'm not stupid enough to try and take him alone. Tonight I won't be alone. It's better than having him come upon me when no one else is around."

"Damn it! Can't you just listen to reason?"

She sighed. "You and George. Who appointed you guys my knights in shining armor?"

"Don't try to change the subject. And who's George?"

Sam's jealousy warmed her heart. "He's my partner. I'll introduce you next chance I get."

"Fine. Do that." He paused. "Please, sweetheart, I'm asking you for a favor. Don't go out there tonight."

Emotion swelled in her throat. Beth swallowed it, then managed the words. "I have to." She heard a crash on the other end of the line, the sound of breaking plaster.

"Damn it all to hell!"

"Sam?"

"Okay. Do this. Risk your life. But while you're at it, keep this little thought under your hat. I'll be watching out for you. Like it or not, I'll protect you if need be."

"No. I told you I don't want you out there. You're a civilian. Strong as you are, you don't know how to handle yourself in this kind of situation."

His voice held the hint of a growl. "You can't tame me like some kind of pet dog. I do what I want. Evidently, I'm as stubborn as you."

"Please, stay home. I want you safe."

His voice softened, the sound of it sending shivers up her spine and heat somewhere else. "Then you know how I feel. I couldn't live with myself if I let anything happen to you."

"I want this over, Sam. I want to be with you."

"Don't go."

"Sorry, that isn't an option."

"Then, for God's sake, be careful. I'll see you tonight."

Beth heard the click of his handset, a dial tone. She hung up the phone, then pulled out the killer's profile to study once more. The written text sprang out at her, reminding her of the terrifying threat that was the Ripper. The hand holding the file began to shake.

"I hope I live that long," she whispered.

Sam stood by the terrace doors and cursed the gathering darkness. Things were moving strobe light fast, out of his control and he felt like a character in a two-bit horror flick. Hunger gnawed at his stomach to underline the reality of the creature inside him. And, for once, he felt grateful. Only someone with his unnatural powers could protect Beth tonight.

But first he must feed.

He went to the bar and pushed the button. Removed the plastic container of blood from the hidden refrigerator. Heated it in the microwave, wondering why the life giving properties in the blood were unaffected by its heating. He tipped it back, drinking deeply. *The blood is the life.* Truer words had never been written. With great gulps, he drained it dry. Then he prepared another.

A gut-wrenching feeling tore at him. He would need all his strength to fight for the woman he loved.

Hand on her hip, breasts thrust forward, Beth slinked into the squad room doing her best parody of a Hollywood movie siren playing a hooker. Wolf-whistles and catcalls made the room sound like a strip bar. Praise from her enthusiastic colleagues—she couldn't help but smile. She did look like a two-dollar bargain in her long platinum-blonde wig. Crushed red velvet clung to every curve of her body, molding to her like a second skin. She wore black nylons held up by a black lace garter belt accentuated by tiny red ribbon rosebuds. Her shoes were red with very spiked heels. There was no way she could run in shoes like these, but, if worse came to worse, she could kick them off and run in her stocking feet. And they might come in handy as extra weapons.

"Very nice, Andrews," Aikens said. "I'd go for you myself if we didn't have this job to do."

Beth laughed. The captain wasn't known for his subtlety. He knew a little humor went a long way to diffuse a bad case of nerves. She played along, pouting as she batted her eyelashes and said in her most sultry voice, "I know, Captain. Perhaps we can make time...later."

He did the most unlikely thing. Like a dad, in front of everyone, rough old Captain Bob Aikens leaned over and planted a kiss on her well made-up cheek. "Be careful out there. I want you back alive," he said so only she could hear.

He pulled back with a leer and raised his voice to include the others. "Time to go to work. Our boys are planted all over the streets thicker than trees in a tropical rain forest. Keep in sight, Andrews. We don't want any mishaps."

Beth checked her bag to make sure it still held her gun. So far, so good. She tilted her head back, took a long, calming breath and released it slowly. She only hoped her good fortune would hold.

GET IT NOW

MyBookStoreAndMore.com

GREAT EBOOKS, GREAT DEALS . . . AND MORE!

Don't wait to run to the bookstore down the street, or
waste time shopping online at one of the "big boys." Now,
all your favorite Samhain authors are all in one place—at
MyBookStoreAndMore.com. Stop by today and discover
great deals on Samhain—and a whole lot more!

WWW.SAMHAINPUBLISHING.COM

hot stuff

Discover Samhain!

THE HOTTEST NEW PUBLISHER ON THE PLANET

Romance, fantasy, mystery, thriller, mainstream and
more—Samhain has more selection, hotter authors, and
everything's available in both ebook and print.

Pick your favorite, sit back, and enjoy the ride!
Hot stuff indeed.

WWW.SAMHAINPUBLISHING.COM

LaVergne, TN USA
15 July 2010
189666LV00004B/80/P